Enchanting
Easter

On Newsstands Now:

TRUE STORY
and
TRUE CONFESSIONS
Magazines

True Story and *True Confessions* are the world's largest and best-selling women's romance magazines. They offer true-to-life stories to which women can relate.

Since 1919, the iconic *True Story* has been an extraordinary publication. The magazine gets its inspiration from the hearts and minds of women, and touches on those things in life that a woman holds close to her heart, like love, loss, family and friendship.

True Confessions, a cherished classic first published in 1922, looks into women's souls and reveals their deepest secrets.

To subscribe, please visit our website:
www.TrueRenditionsLLC.com or call **(212) 922-9244**

To find the TRUES at your local store, please visit:
www.WheresMyMagazine.com

Enchanting Easter

From the Editors
Of *True Story* And
True Confessions

Published by True Renditions, LLC

True Renditions, LLC
105 E. 34th Street, Suite 141
New York, NY 10016

ISBN: 978-1-938877-93-3

Visit us on the web at www.truerenditionsllc.com.

Contents

SCAVENGER HUNT

Mommy!"

I sat straight up in bed, momentarily startled and not knowing where I happened to be. Within seconds it sank in—Sunday morning. I'd finally been able to sleep in. I looked at the clock. No, I guess I hadn't slept in. As I watched, the numbers clicked over to the regular waking time of seven a.m.

Lauren bounced up on the bed, her bedraggled bunny rabbit clutched in one hand.

"Look out the window, Mommy."

Lauren was my pride, my joy, and the reason I'd stayed sane after my husband died two years ago, and right now she was bright-eyed and ready to play. I gave a mental sigh. I looked longingly at my pillow, but had no time to dive back under the covers.

"Come on, Mommy," she urged, pulling at my hand. "Look out the window."

I shoved back blankets, rubbed my eyes, ran a hand through messy hair, staggered to the window, and stared.

Several dozen brightly colored plastic Easter eggs hung from our big oak tree. I could see others peeping out behind bushes, the rock-lined driveway, and my little picket fence.

Of course, I'd forgotten it was Easter Sunday. My plan had been to sleep in as long as I could and get up in time to go to our church services, and then let Lauren do the Easter Egg Hunt the church had planned, since I hadn't had time to do something at home.

Kevin's life insurance had allowed me to buy a small house and put money into savings for Lauren's college fund, but I had to work to provide for Lauren and myself—not that I was complaining. I loved my job as a nurse, and helping people just made me feel good. But this past month we'd been swamped with injuries and were shorthanded, so I actually worked overtime.

Thank goodness my neighbor Noah had been home; he babysat Lauren on days when I ran late.

"The Easter Bunny did it." Lauren informed me sagely. She shrugged up an arm with the ragged bunny hanging limply over it. "Gordon's brother."

I gave Gordon a skeptical look. I very much doubted her bunny had anything to do with the decorations in my yard. But with six-year-olds, one had to be careful about some facts since innocence was at stake. I frowned as my sluggish brain finally connected. I hadn't done the decorations.

1

So who did? My parents lived across town, but I was pretty sure my mother would've told me if she had something planned. My boss lived three blocks away but I didn't think he would have thought of something like this. Or would he? Last year, for Lauren's fifth birthday, he'd sent a singing clown with balloons to her. I had to work overtime and was upset that Lauren wouldn't understand. Colton saved the day by making it special for my little girl. Recently divorced, he'd worked hard to spend time with his own two children, so he understood better than most that parents didn't always have time.

I scratched my head and yawned.

Of course, that was when Scout, the golden Labrador Retriever went racing by, quickly followed by his master, Noah.

I cringed. I looked down at the T-shirt I was wearing, and cringed again. It was one Kevin had given me for Valentine's Day a couple years before he died. "TAKE ME, I'M YOURS!" it screamed in big red letters over my chest.

Noah already thought I was the klutzy neighbor lady, and our two-year history had done nothing to dispel his misgivings about me. When I first came to look at the house with the real estate agent, she had transposed numbers and mistaken his house for the one we were to look at. The lawn sign was staked on the edge of the property, so it was a natural mistake. However, she'd been brusque to him and it went downhill from there for a while.

The first year, I backed into his garbage cans. Then our cat walked the fence between our yards, and Noah's dog Scout leapt over a four-foot fence he'd never known he could jump. He dodged cars, bikes, and an in-line skater as a herd of people tried to catch him or the cat. Our neighbors still talked about the circus antics as Sally and Scout streaked through yards, trees, and one house. Several of them claimed we should've sold tickets. Noah had to lengthen the fence to five feet with chicken wire so Scout wouldn't get out again.

Then Lauren picked all of the flowers off Noah's rosebush one Mother's Day to give to me. Then there was the time she crawled into the car after a doll she'd left behind, kicked the gearshift, rolled my car across Noah's driveway, and knocked him over as he watered his lawn.

This year, we'd finally worked out a truce. I made cookies as often as possible with my busy schedule. I watched Noah's animals, including Scout, two cats, the rabbit, and the fish when Noah was away on business trips, and I had the man over for the occasional thank-you dinner when he mowed my lawn, unclogged my sink, or babysat Lauren for a few minutes. I hoped it changed his opinion, but sometimes he had a quizzical half-smile on his face when he saw me, and I knew he was remembering those other times.

He waved and continued his run.

2

Thank goodness it was only Noah. There are some men you feel so comfortable with, it doesn't matter what you're wearing—or what you look like, for that matter.

"Can we go out, Mommy?"

I gave my snuggly bed one last look of longing and nodded.

Ten minutes later, I was dressed decently, had my hair in a ponytail, and at least managed to brush my teeth.

Lauren nearly ran down Sally as she raced into the yard, and I followed, still wondering who loved my child enough to make her this happy. Lauren was collecting the eggs that were at ground level, rooting under the petunias and plucking them out of the fence rails. As she found the eggs, she opened them to find little treats inside. A pink bead necklace draped from her fingers as the next egg revealed a small whistle. Before I could stop her, she blew it loud and long. Jack, my neighbor across the street, looked as he picked up his newspaper, grinned at the eggs hanging on my tree, and waved as he went back into his house. His wife, Maisie, was known for her baking, and I wondered if she had made her famous pecan coffeecake because of the speed with which Jack had disappeared.

"This one's for you, Mommy," Lauren sang, as she waved a pastel blue egg at me.

For me? My daughter was confused; adults didn't do egg hunts.

I held out my hand and she plopped the two halves into it. A small piece of paper fluttered out exactly the same size as a fortune cookie note.

I squinted and read the note.

"For a flame-haired Mommy, a gift of fun/ look outside the fence for a purple one."

"What's it say, Mommy?" Lauren came running back, her shirt cupped as she cradled more eggs.

"I thought you read it?" I said, wondering how she knew it was for me.

"No, I saw the Mommy word and just gave it to you."

"It says I have to look outside the fence for a purple egg."

She ran to the one-foot-high picket fence that framed the driveway and looked over it, scanning the length.

"There it is!"

With a sense of wonder, I reached down and picked up the egg. I cracked the halves, and another note fell out into my hand.

"A merry chase, a smile in place/check the oak for the color of yolk."

"It's a treasure hunt, Mommy." Lauren nudged her head close to read my note. "For you! And all the other eggs are for me!" She squealed and was off again to find more eggs.

3

I looked at the eggs hanging from the oak tree—only one was yellow.

I looked around my neighborhood, but no one seemed to be watching the little drama unfolding in my front yard.

Who on earth had planned something like this for Lauren, and for me? Was it a joke? Would my neighbors jump out of the bushes at the last egg and scream, 'Happy Easter!'?" We were a friendly crowd, having picnics and barbeques together during the summer months— we even decorated our entire street for Christmas together. Our themed lights and lawn ornaments had won the city's lights contest the two years Lauren and I had lived here. Many of my neighbors knew I worked hard, and I wondered if they knew my time constraints. I felt a rush of camaraderie for my friends. Of course, they'd planned this for Lauren and me, knowing I'd been busy these past few months.

I walked to the oak tree with a smile on my face.

"Jellybeans in this one, Mommy," Lauren yelled as she was stuffing them in her mouth. "They even have a note that says they're sugar-free."

I felt another rush of warmth for my friends. That had to be MaryAnn's idea. She lived two doors down and one of her sons was a diabetic. Rather than make him feel different, she simply adjusted kid-friendly recipes that anyone could eat and bought sugar-free candy for all the kids at Halloween.

I reached up and untied the yellow egg from the branches.

"Of gifts and games, I have too few/ but for a date, look for two blues."

Shock reverberated all the way to my toes.

A date? Someone was asking me out on a date?

I stood there astounded, too surprised to even think for a couple of minutes. Lauren was zipping around the yard, picking up eggs, opening them, and playing with the little trinkets inside. She turned a gap-toothed grin to me and waved. My child was having the time of her life and someone, someone who knew us well, was asking me out, and they knew me well enough to know that Lauren was important in my life, well enough to give my child a treat at the same time they— no he—wanted to know if I would go out on a date.

Now my thoughts were complicated; conflicting emotions reigned. I'd not dated since Kevin died. I'd not even been interested for a long time. But life had resumed, and even though a little knot of grief pierced my heart at the oddest times, mostly I was content that I would always have Kevin's child, a remembrance of my loving husband, to cherish.

Was I ready to date?

I didn't even know; it hadn't occurred to me to find out.

4

I laughed a little. Obviously, this man—whoever he was—hadn't seen me this morning hanging out my window with bed-head and a ratty T-shirt that had seen better days. Dating material I was not.

With that thought, I ran through the list of men whom I came in contact with that professed interest. Sadly, that list was short. Actually it was non-existent. I couldn't figure out who wanted to ask me out. I wracked my brain but could think of no clues to lead me to a conclusion. No one had seemed the slightest bit interested in me except in a professional or neighborly way—unless my date-detector genes had totally failed. It was possible, I supposed.

Wait. A date. Maybe it wasn't about dating a man. Maybe it was an important date someone wanted me to remember, like a birthday or an anniversary. A vague sense of disappointment feathered through my heart, and I realized that I was ready to date. I was ready to begin a relationship with a man again. Maybe it wouldn't go anywhere or maybe it would, but the knowledge made me smile a little as I contemplated dinners, picnics, and interests with someone I liked. It'd been too long since I'd had time to enjoy something with someone special. With a small sigh, I knew that although I'd always remember and love Kevin, his life was beyond me now and I could learn to love again. With a slight touch of sadness, I had finally let Kevin go.

I glanced around the yard, remembering the note's contents. What anniversary had I forgotten? What date did the mysterious treasure hunt maker want me to know?

Peeking out from under the petunias on the far side of the driveway, I saw the two blue eggs.

I looked around my neighborhood again; no one was in sight, no curtains fluttered. At the end of the block I saw Noah and Scout turning to go run the path at the park, but other than them, no one was outside.

My thoughts turned back to my mother. Had I forgotten my parents' anniversary? No. I sent a card and tickets to the Saturday matinee for them. My mother and father had met at the theater, she as a ticket salesperson, and he as the popcorn man. In one of her too-much-information conversations with me once, she said she and Dad loved going to the Saturday matinee to make out in the dark, just like old times. Naturally, this grossed me out, but I figured as long as I didn't have to witness my parents being goo-goo-eyed at each other, I could spring for tickets. Mom had laughed and told me later it was a great gift, especially since she and Dad shocked the nearby teenagers who were being too noisy.

I picked up the two eggs. A number one was painted on the first, and a number two was painted on the second. Being the radical incendiary that I was, I opened the number two first.

"Aha, I say, I knew you would/ open number two before you should."

Well dang, someone really knew me well. I wondered if Dad was in on this—the man teased me incessantly most of my life. I teased him, too, just to get back at him.

I could see Lauren sitting on the porch with her loot, showing Sally what she'd collected so far. The cat sniffed each offering with a delicate air before turning away with disinterest.

I opened the number one egg.

"A special flower, called Angel Face/harbors a pink egg at its base."

It took me a couple of seconds to remember that I had a blue rose called Angel Face in my side yard. I walked towards my feeble attempt of a rose garden, three bushes I'd bought at the nursery last year.

"Where are you going, Mommy?" Lauren had left her collected eggs on the porch and was going into the yard to get more.

"My clue says I have to go find a pink egg under the rose bush."

"Oh. Can I get the eggs out of the tree now?" She turned to look at them.

"Only the ones you can reach. I'll come back and help you with the higher ones."

"Okay!" She skipped off on her own treasure hunt.

The pink egg was placed carefully enough that no thorns scratched my hand as I took it from near the roots.

"As Lady Luck will have her way/ a shamrock egg will show the way."

A green egg. I laughed to myself at the poet's attempt to be original with his colors. I saw the green egg stuck in the chicken wire of Scout's fence.

I had a passing thought that the person who'd arranged this hunt was clever about making sure Lauren wouldn't or couldn't get to my eggs. Once again, the thoughtfulness gave me a pause; someone had spent time and effort on our behalf to make this fun.

"Around the front and down the lane/ we're back to using purple again."

I got the first part, but 'down the lane'?

For a few seconds I stood in front of my house. . .The driveway—of course! I trotted down the driveway and saw the purple egg, right under my mailbox.

"Closer now, you're getting there/ look for an egg, the color of a pear."

Once again I scanned my yard and the sidewalk, looking for another egg. A flash of yellow popped in my peripheral vision. Nestled between the branches of the oak was an egg. It wasn't hanging like the others, and I could only see it if I was standing exactly where I stood.

6

I gave my mystery person credit for imagination.

"Oh wonderful day, hip-hip, hooray!/ Sky blue is the color of the day!"

I laughed. The mystery writer was getting close to the end, I was sure of it.

A hanging basket on the edge of my porch had the blue egg peeking over the top.

"Lauren's busy having fun/ one more pink egg, then one purple till done!"

I saw the pink egg first. This time it was squarely in the center of my porch mums, balanced on one of the sturdy flowers.

"Cat hair and fins, fur and bark. . ." The poem ended before the last line. Now that was funny. . .

The mention of animals had me slightly worried. Lauren wanted a dog, but so far I'd held off until my schedule would give us time to properly care for one. I hoped my parents, or whoever this mystery person was, hadn't planned to give us a puppy for our treasure. Despite the fun, I'd have to refuse the gift. With that thought, a little of the light went out of my day; I hoped I'd not have to disappoint someone. I'd better find out.

The purple egg had to be around here somewhere.

Lauren had hauled another pile of eggs to the porch. She'd managed to get them all out of the tree. I checked the ground, the flowers, the path, and the driveway.

"What are you looking for, Mommy?"

"A purple egg."

She got up and began looking with me. We searched the side yard by the rose bushes, the front of the picket fence, the spaces between the paved rocks of the driveway. We looked in all the flowerpots on the front porch, the cushions of my porch chairs, and under the seat covers on the swing. Lauren scrabbled under the petunias and in the bushes.

"Looking for this?" Noah, his hair still damp from a shower, stood in his yard, holding a purple egg. That half-quizzical smile was on his face again. Scout sat beside him, attentive and alert.

A myriad of emotions assailed me as the glimmer of truth dawned. I gingerly took the egg from his hand and cracked the halves.

"A dinner date for three, at Noah's Ark?"

I smiled; Noah grinned. Lauren laughed and danced. Scout barked, and Sally viewed the humans and their silly eggs with deep disdain.

We were married three months later in the front yard, with eggs hanging from the tree and scattered around my yard, just like the treasure hunt that started it all.

THE END

CRASH INTO LOVE

Becka's Blooms, Please Come In! read the unlit neon sign in the window of my shop. I was anxious to plug in this new addition to the window as I pulled my economy car around to the back of the building, for these were the only kind of lights that I ever wanted to see my name in. At last, I was making enough money to take my business to the next level, to afford a cute new sign, to advertise in a larger area, and maybe even to trade in my old Nissan for a new model.

These were my thoughts as I entered my business through the rear door, my chest filling with pride because whenever I completed this simple act, it reminded me that I had followed my dream. Today, it was even better because things were going so well.

I remembered how so many people had told me I could be "so much more than a florist." College professors had tried to push me in the direction of teaching and the field of law, and my parents had encouraged me to go to medical school. But flowers had thrilled me for as long as I could remember, and in spite of all these urgings to seek other careers, I had gone to community college to get a junior degree in business and had saved up to open my own flower shop. I looked forward to a busy day, as the Easter season was upon the small city of Danville and the orders for spring party arrangements were rolling in.

I would be making some deliveries to a few houses in the elite section of town that day and would leave my office assistant, Karen, in charge of the store. My customers had spent an ample amount of money on their flowers, and there was no doubt in my mind that they expected perfection. I didn't want to trust the delivery to anyone else because, naturally, I wanted the return business of high-end clients.

I looked around at the inside of my shop as I always did, said hello to my roses and daisies and carnations and babies breath—all my most used flowers, and the best friends of my business. Everything was in place for a busy day, the arrangements were waiting in the cooler to be loaded into my company van, and Karen walked through the door right on time, talking to one of her teenaged children on her cell phone momentarily. The day was falling into place, like any other, but with a little more excitement—Easter was only a day away and spring was indeed beginning to spring. Before unlocking the front door and flipping over the sign that read, Yes, We're Open! Please Come In! Karen and I loaded up the van for my trip to the Rolling Hills section of town.

"I should be back by noontime. If not, just go ahead and lock up for an hour and take lunch," I told Karen.

"Oh, I'm sure you'll be back in time and if you're not, I'll just wait," Karen said like she always did, one of the reasons we worked so well together. Karen really understood the do's and don'ts of business and aspired to open a daycare center in town in the future. the importance of keeping good relationships with the local people was not lost on her.

"Thanks, Karen. See you soon," I called from the window of the van as I drove away.

The cool, crisp air of the April morning chilled but excited me, and the morning dew made everything sparkle and shine. I loved this time of the year and was also looking forward to seeing the insides of some spectacular houses in Rolling Hills. I didn't often go to that section of town unless I had specific business there, but whenever I did, I was amazed at the mix of old Victorians and colonials and the new versions of the same styles. The flowers, landscaping, and gardens thrilled me, and I was awed by how old met new in the area and how it all seemed to work so well together. That day was no different. I even entertained the notion that someday I might be able to afford to live in one of the smaller houses in Rolling Hills. But then I said out loud, "Becka, who are you fooling? You knew when you followed your dream that it would not lead you to Rolling Hills!" My disappointment never lasted long because I quickly remembered how happy I was with my decision to listen to my heart instead of my wallet. Nevertheless, I looked up and back at the beautiful homes lining George Street as I checked for number forty-eight, my first stop in the area. George Street was probably the prettiest street of all, as it bordered a state forest and was where the hills really did "roll," for all of the houses were built on a slope and had fabulous front yards. If it was summer, landscapers would be mowing and trimming, and the owners of the houses would be out planting or tending their flowers, but even in spring the lawns were perfect with hardly a stray fallen leaf leftover from autumn to be seen.

I turned my head to the left to look at one of my favorite houses, a hulking Victorian painted in soft greens and yellows. As I turned completely back to the road, I saw, with horror, that the driver of a black BMW convertible was aggressively pulling out in front of me from one of the houses on the other side of the road, and that he had a cell phone pressed to his face. I shrieked, because he was obviously not even paying attention to what he was doing and was not even looking in my direction. There was no doubt that we would crash, and I braced myself for the impact, thinking more about my precious flower arrangements in the back of the van than I was thinking about myself.

At the last minute, the man driving the car saw me and tried to swerve to avoid me, but it was a fruitless effort; his shiny black car slammed broadside into my white van. The hit could not have been in a worse place; I knew all of my hard work was being destroyed. I thought something silly: If only he could have hit the front of the van! For even if I landed in the hospital, Karen could have delivered the flowers unharmed to my customers. My heart was hurt more than my body was. Shaking, I got out of the van to look at the damage and to be sure that the BMW's driver was not injured.

Quite the contrary, for the very handsome man with thick black hair and dark, wild eyes was jumping out of the car, snapping his cell phone closed, and stomping over in my direction looking like he wanted to slap me.

"What are you thinking, Ms. Becka's Blooms? Look at the mess you've caused!" He bellowed.

I stopped in my tracks and stared at him in disbelief. "What are you talking about? I didn't cause anything. You were talking on a cell phone and weren't even looking. All I was doing was driving down the street trying to find a customer's house." My voice was shaking, and I honestly didn't know where it was coming from. I didn't get into conflicts like this with people very often, and I was not accustomed to having someone yell at me. The first time my previous boyfriend had raised his voice to me, I had ended our relationship after a year of dating because I knew what that behavior could eventually lead to. I chose not to have people like him and this man in my life. I lived very quietly with my family close by, my flowers, a tiny Chihuahua named Tex, and some nice friends that were quiet like me.

"Well, I live here, and I don't appreciate some two-bit florist talking back to me in front of my own home," he lashed out.

This man was so handsome, and yet the ugliness and foolishness that came out of his mouth made him look utterly unattractive to me. I wondered what it mattered that he lived in the stately house just up the hill from our accident when it was him that had not even looked to see if anyone was coming down the street and it was him that had been talking on a cell phone instead of paying attention to his driving.

And whom exactly was he calling a two-bit florist? Who did he think he was? I glanced at the mailbox at the bottom of the steep drive that led to the top of the hill. The box read Staley and did not mean anything to me when I first saw it.

Mr. Staley was ranting about how he didn't have time for such stupidity and how he would sue me for keeping him away from his office in town. He opened his phone again to call the police, and when he told the dispatcher he was "Norman Staley, the CPA on Front Street," I started to get an idea of whom I was dealing with.

One of my good friends who was recently married had told me about Norman Staley and had described him as "sexy and reckless." She had dated him even though everyone in town knew he had a gorgeous blond fiancé from Sweden. My friend had stopped seeing him for the same reason I had broken up with my boyfriend: she reported Norman had a temper that he had a hard time controlling. Later we would find out he was the spoiled rich son of a family that had been in Danville for one hundred years and had lived in Rolling Hills since long before it had become the exclusive area it was now. He had a reputation around town for being a brilliant CPA, but was very hard to deal with because of his superior attitude. These bits of information came back to me as I tried to distance myself from him to wait out the formalities of our accident. I managed to do just that but only until he was done on the phone. Shutting it once again, he came at me.

"The police are on their way. If I were you, I wouldn't mention the fact that I was on my phone when we had our little crash."

Our little crash? Not tell the police the truth? What was this man thinking? Already I felt I knew what was going through his head: he had money and was good-looking and well known in town, so he was trying to intimidate me, a petite blond who was, in his eyes, a lowly florist. I did feel somewhat intimidated by all of these factors, but my main emotion was anger, because he thought all of these things were so important. Yet what angered me the most was that he had destroyed my hard work, and because of him, I would likely lose the high-end clientele that I had felt so good about attaining. Because of Norman Staley, I would potentially lose what I had worked so hard to get and I would miss out on customers who could really make a difference for my business and my finances.

A few stray pink and yellow rose petals came wafting out of the smashed small side window of my shop van and onto the pavement. I watched as the cool breeze blew them around, yet I did not want to look at what was inside the van because I already knew what I would see, and for me it would have been like seeing someone I loved torn and bleeding after a crash.

"Do you think I'm going to lie to the police for you? When you smash into me and ruin all of the flowers that I was delivering to people that trusted me?" I felt my fury rising, for I may have been five-foot-two, but my parents always said I had six-foot-four of temper if you rubbed me the wrong way. So, Norman Staley had some competition when I got heated up! I felt plain insulted by his attitude and the fact that he expected me to lie to a law enforcement official to save face for him after how he had talked to me.

"Well, I'm just warning you. I'm really well-known in this town and you're just looking for trouble saying anything against me."

"Are you threatening me?" I demanded.

"No, it's not a threat. Just consider it a warning. And it was just a bunch of stupid flowers anyway. Look at what I did to my car because of you. Do you know how much this car cost me?"

I had to turn away from him to contain my rage, telling myself that if I wasn't careful, I would get myself arrested. Then my business would be in real trouble. I realized I needed to call the three customers in the area that would be without flowers because of "our little crash," as Norman Staley had so charmingly put it. I took out my cell phone, where I had their numbers stored.

"And just who are you calling?" Norman Staley looked and sounded nervous.

"It's none of your business who I'm calling. At least I waited until I stopped driving before I started making phone calls!" I snapped, and walked away from him. I knew I sounded confident, but my heart was going a mile a minute. I was surprised that my voice wasn't shaking, because the rest of me certainly was!

Iris Fenton was the first customer I called. She lived a mere three houses down from Staley House, as it was named on a black iron filigree signpost in front of it. Iris was more concerned about me than the flowers and wondered if there was anything she could do to help.

"No, it's okay. A local hit me and he has already called the police."

"A local? Who, dear?" she asked.

"Um. . ." I wondered if I should tell her, fearing vengeance from the rich Cormans. But I decided to tell her and see what her reaction would be. "Norman Staley."

"Oh, dear. Watch out for that one. He's ruthless."

So now I had another adjective to describe Norman. Sexy, reckless, ruthless—a real charmer!

My other two customers were also understanding, more concerned about me than my flowers. I told them all that I would do anything in my power to get them replacement arrangements. The last call I made was to Karen.

"Karen, this is Becka. I was in an accident and the flowers were destroyed but I'm okay. Close the shop and start making any arrangement that you can with what we have in Easter colors. I'll be back as soon as I can to help you." I told her I didn't have time to explain, but to call my parents and tell them I would need a ride home from Rolling Hills. The police siren was getting near as I hung up the phone.

A kindly middle-aged police officer named Harris arrived moments later followed by an ambulance, which would not be utilized but was sent as a precaution. I was relieved to see the familiar officer; he came

12

in often to buy flowers for his wife. I knew he would give me a fair shake. Norman Staley glowered at me when Officer Harris called me by my first name. I felt as though I had an advantage over him now and decided I would not tell Officer Harris how he had been talking on his cell phone. It was already quite clear to me that in spite of the fact that Norman had been trying to influence the dispatcher over the phone by using his name and title, justice would be served.

I was correct; he was cited for reckless driving. I couldn't help but smile to myself when I thought of how my friend Tawny had described him to me as "reckless."

My father showed up as a tow truck was taking our vehicles away. The good news was that my van would be able to be repaired. The bad news was that I still had three desirable customers to satisfy in the next eighteen hours. Dad wanted to bring me to the hospital to check and be sure I had not suffered any invisible injuries, but I begged him to bring me back to the shop and he finally agreed.

"Just can't keep you away from those flowers, can we?" he quipped.

"No, Dad. It's impossible!" I tried to smile even though I was still shaken up by the accident and perhaps even more so by the way that awful Norman Staley spoke me to.

Dad shook his head. "I'm worried about the repercussions from that—that—" He struggled to find a word to describe Norman.

I leaned over to the driver's side of his SUV to kiss his cheek. "Don't worry. Maybe nothing will come of it," I said. But I was as worried as him. "I may need your truck tomorrow to make deliveries. And tell Mom I'll be late for Easter dinner." I jumped out of the comfortable Ford before he could object.

Karen was waiting at the front door and let me in immediately, demanding the full story of what had happened to me.

"Norman Staley!" she shrieked, as if I had just told her that Jack the Ripper had hit me. "My husband was in the same graduating class as him, and even he said he's a total jerk!"

Clearly, Norman didn't have much of a fan club. But I hoped that somewhere along the way someone was going to say something nice about him so I wouldn't have to worry about him coming after me or my business. Even as I thought this, I calculated that he was six years older than me, as I knew Karen's husband was thirty-five. Thirty-five: old enough to know better than to act the way he had acted after our accident. As Karen and I continued to create the replacement arrangements she had already started, I itched to have Norman standing in front of me again so I could give him a piece of my mind. Soon enough though, I forgot about him as I lost myself in the task at hand.

Karen and I worked feverishly until ten that night and managed to make some pretty nice arrangements for the customers in Rolling Hills. The next morning, which was Easter, I called my father to ask if I could use his truck.

"No, you can't. I'll pick you up at home, we'll go to the shop together to load everything, and I'll do the driving!" He said with fatherly consternation.

"Well, I'm ready whenever you are." I appreciated Dad's help and concern and was glad he had offered it.

The trip back down George Street was very strange for me, and when we passed the Staley house, I looked at it up on the hill, impressive and dignified, unlike at least one of its occupants. The driveway was full of cars, and I imagined a bunch of rich people sitting around a huge table and Norman laughing as he told them how he had hit a florist who was barely over five feet tall and how he would sue her and put her out of business.

Iris Fenton was thrilled with her flowers, and I had to admit, in the heat of the moment, Karen and I had gotten extra creative with what we had.

"I don't know how you managed to pull this off, Ms. Ingram, but I'm extremely impressed," Iris said with a smile.

"Oh, it was nothing," I said, weary because I was exhausted from working so long and hard, but also because I couldn't stop thinking how the Staley family would probably come after me and ruin everything I had worked for over the past four years since I had opened my shop. I could see the house from one of Iris's windows, and I peered over at it.

As if reading my mind, Iris said, "Don't worry about Norman Staley, dear. He makes a lot of threats but doesn't follow through on them."

The things people were telling me about him seemed to get worse instead of better! But I was actually relieved by what Iris said, and on the next two deliveries I was able to put the whole situation out of my mind once again and just be happy that I was able to save some face with my customers in Rolling Hills. Later, I celebrated Easter with my parents and my older brother and was hoping to get back to business as usual the next day.

The following week was extremely busy, not only from deliveries and walk-ins, but also with the orders coming in for spring flowers. There were even two new customers from Rolling Hills who had been to Iris's house and seen her Easter arrangements. She had given me an excellent referral, even though I had convinced myself there would be a "Becka's Blooms backlash" in Rolling Hills after my accident with Norman Staley. I had not forgotten about him; whenever the phone rang or the bell on the door tinkled, I feared it would be him on the other end of the connection or striding across the floor. However, it wasn't actually until two weeks after our accident, when I had started to forget about the whole scene, that he decided to show up, sending a shudder through me. I was alone in the shop and immediately wished I had not let Karen go home early.

"Good afternoon, Ms. Ingram," he said with some kindness, yet still with an edge to his voice that I didn't trust.

"May I help you?" I asked, all business, only meeting his eyes for a single beat, for they were amazing almond-brown eyes, and I was afraid if I looked into them for too long I would forget they belonged to a complete jerk.

Norman faltered at my tone and started looking very uncomfortable. He ran his hand through his thick, dark hair and sighed. "Ms. Ingram, I came to apologize for the problem we had a couple of weeks back. I know it was my fault, and I'm glad I was cited for it."

I almost didn't hear what he said, for all the negative emotions from that awful day started to come back to me. I remembered how I had imagined him standing in front of me and had practiced all the things I would spit at him through clenched teeth. Now was my chance, and suddenly, though I had not thought about the whole thing in over a week, I wanted my chance to tear him apart as he had done to me.

"You asked me to lie to a police officer, you degraded me and my profession, and now you come to apologize to me?" I hissed, my teeth together just like I had imagined.

"I degraded you and your profession?" Norman was clearly taken aback.

And so was I, needing to explain how he had thought his car was so much more important than my flowers!

"You don't remember saying that?" I was losing my anger and was feeling silly for the way I was acting. My parents would be appalled that I didn't just accept his apology and send him on his way. Even my father, knowing Norman's reputation in town, would tell me to let the anger go because what was done was done and of course he would be right.

"Actually, Ms. Ingram, I don't. Hospice had come in that day to take care of my mother and I don't know where my mind was. I'm sure I said a lot of things that I would want back in my mouth. I was honestly just trying to escape that situation, and well, you unfortunately got in the way."

Norman was over six feet tall and was quite imposing. But when his broad shoulders were slumped, as they were then, he looked much less daunting.

"Oh, I—I'm sorry." Now I felt downright foolish. "Is she—?"

He shook his head, knowing my question. "No, she died on Easter."

I had a vision of going by the Staley House on Easter Sunday when Dad and I were making my deliveries. Seeing all the cars in the driveway, I had been sure there was a great party going on under that magnificent roof and that I was the laughing stock.

"I'm really sorry," I admitted.

He brightened a little. "I got my car back yesterday. Did you get your van fixed?"

"Yes, it's all set."

I cringed as Norman looked around my shop, but he did so with interested eyes.

"This is a great little place. I've always loved flowers. My mother and father both had an appreciation for them. I would have asked you to do her funeral arrangements, but I didn't think you would after. . ." His voice drifted off.

"Of course I would have done them. It's not in my business plan to turn away customers."

"I'll remember that next time I need flowers. Well, I have to get back to the office." At the door, he turned back to me and asked, "Listen, would you like to go for coffee sometime?"

I felt so strange standing there with this man whom I had heard so many terrible things about looking at me like I had caught him with his hand in the cookie jar, shuffling his feet and asking me, the lowly florist, to have coffee with him. I could already hear the protests from my father, my friend Tawny, Karen and her husband, so I said, "No, I don't think that would be a good idea," though if I was thinking for myself, the answer would have been much different. Norman seemed sincerely sorry. Furthermore, he was sexy and not-so-ruthless, and to me, that was the perfect combination!

He nodded. "I thought you would say that." He lifted his hand to me in a gesture of goodbye with a little bit of defeat mixed in before he disappeared.

Norman's visit bothered me for days after that, but I didn't speak with anyone about it. Finally, a week later, Karen made the observation that I had been really quiet, and I decided to confide in her as we were going over our orders for spring arrangements.

To my surprise, she was not totally shocked by my revelation.

"I've been hearing from people around town that Norman is acting a lot differently since his mother passed away. I hear his father has Alzheimer's, and it's gotten so bad he is in Edgewater Nursing Home now. So, Norman is living all alone in the family house in Rolling Hills."

"What about the fiancé from Sweden?" The answer to this question had been bothering me since he had asked me out. I couldn't bear the thought that he, or any man, would proposition me behind the back of another woman.

"Oh, he broke up with her last year."

16

Hearing this offered me some relief, as did the fact that Karen voiced some good thoughts about Norman. I wasn't sure what it all meant to me, however, considering I had turned him down for coffee and therefore would probably never come in contact with him again. My worries turned out to be fruitless though, for a couple of days after Karen and I had this conversation, Norman returned to Becka's Blooms right after Karen left for the day. This time I had the feeling he had been watching and waiting for her to leave.

"You've probably heard around town that I don't give up easily, Ms. Ingram. I came again to see if you would have that cup of coffee with me," he said sheepishly.

He looked very handsome and casual in a lightweight sweater and jeans. Rays from the late-day sun followed him into the shop. I looked out the front door to see he was driving the very car he had slammed into my van with, all shiny and perfect once again. I wasn't sure I could get into that car, or that I could trust Norman enough to go anywhere with him in the same vehicle, though I really did want to have coffee with him and see if there was anything nice about him after all the bad things I had heard. I couldn't see what one coffee would hurt.

So, I agreed to meet him at Dana's Deli, a popular meeting place a few streets away from the shop. I asked him to give me an hour to take care of some end-of-the-day business.

"Do you want me to come back and get you?" He asked.

"No, I'll meet you there." I tried not to answer too quickly, lest he might figure out that I did not completely trust him. Norman agreed and left quietly.

While I tied up the day's loose ends around the shop, I wondered if I was doing the right thing by having coffee with Norman. It wasn't really a date, was it? I would pay for my own coffee and would not have anything else, even though I was hungry and I knew the food at Dana's was great. I didn't have any idea what Norman and I would talk about or what we would have in common, being that our backgrounds were totally different. I had grown up modestly and continued to live as such, while he was from an affluent family that had been in town for over a century. But what really stuck in my head was the fact that I didn't trust Norman enough to ride in the same car as him, and I knew trust was the cornerstone of any relationship. Perhaps I should stand him up, not show up at Dana's? Well, he knew where to find me and would likely come back, for he had just told me he didn't give up easily. Reminding myself that I was only having coffee with him and that we would probably never see each other again, I determined to make good on agreeing to meet with him.

I finished my tasks and drove to Dana's, parking right next to Norman's BMW. To my shock, a tall, attractive brunette was standing next to his table when I walked in and was talking to him with a look of sheer adoration on her face. I stopped in my tracks on the way over to him, thinking that this was the kind of woman that was more likely to land Norman Staley than I was: Her clothes were expensive, her hair was perfect, and she looked like she had just had her makeup done by a professional. Instead, he was having coffee with me in my casual clothes, my face plain with just a touch of blusher and lip gloss, my long blond hair pulled back to stay out of my way. The woman was tall like him too and was wearing heels, while I was in flats and was a foot shorter than him. In short, she and I were complete opposites. I thought about turning and leaving, for I could tell him that I had walked in and he had appeared to be "busy" with an admirer. But he saw me and smiled, waving me over. The happiness that had been on the young woman's face melted away as she eyed me up and down before saying a hasty goodbye to Norman and walking off.

"A customer," he explained briefly, and from the way he said it, I knew there would be no further discussion about his visitor. "Order whatever you like." He pushed a menu in my direction and opened one for himself.

"Oh, I'll just have coffee," I said, determined to stick with my plan to not get too comfortable with Norman Staley, especially after finding him talking to another woman.

"Just coffee? With all of this great food on the menu? You can't tell me you don't love the Philly cheese steak sandwich they serve here."

It was only my favorite thing on the menu! My mouth started watering at the thought of having one. I agreed to order one, but told myself I would pay my own bill.

"I heard through the Danville grapevine that you are a very sweet and pretty woman. Unfortunately, I didn't see for myself until we had our accident." Norman caught me off guard while I was still trying to figure out what I would wash down my Philly cheese steak with. He beamed at me over my menu.

"The Danville grapevine?" People in town actually talked about me and the way I looked? I could see if they talked about my touch with flowers or my flawless business practices, but I couldn't imagine that anyone would be interested in my personal attributes.

"Of course, they were completely accurate."

I wondered if I should share what that same grapevine said about him. I decided against it, presuming that he already knew and probably didn't care. Besides, the relaxed way he was talking to me and the gentle smile he gave me didn't fit the descriptions I'd gotten of him. I had to give him a fair shake. Could it be the rumors were false? That he really wasn't what people thought he was? Or perhaps, as Karen had heard, he was changing?

"I know what you're thinking. You've heard a lot about me, and none of it is very nice. And probably a lot of it is true. I have not always had the best of intentions. But you know, since my mother died a few weeks ago, and since we had that accident and I could have really hurt you by being so ignorant, I've opened my eyes to my ways. I've realized that my life isn't going in the right direction. My mother is gone, my father is dying, my fiancé left me over a year ago. . . I was partying a little too much with my buddies at the country club, working a little too hard, just not being very productive."

"Well, I'm glad you're making changes. I have to admit, some of the things I heard about you were not very. . ." I couldn't finish without sounding too harsh.

"Flattering? I know, Ms. Ingram."

I didn't expect that our conversation would get so personal so quickly, or that he would continue to call me "Ms. Ingram."

"Please, call me Becka."

"So, we're friends now?"

A flirty smile played on his lips, and I couldn't help but smile.

"Yes, of course."

"You really forgive me for acting like such a donkey?"

"Well, I understand you were under a lot of stress, so of course I forgive you."

"Good, then I'll keep sending customers your way."

The waitress came with our coffee, a big steaming pot that smelled fresh and enticing. I stared at him questioningly across the table. "Sending. . .?"

"The first time I was in your shop I took some business cards and put them on my desk at my office. Some of my clients took them and said they would be paying you a visit." He named a couple of names and sure enough, they had been in. "And did you also get a call from a fellow named Orson Williams? I sent him over, too."

Orson Williams! He had called that very day and asked for the biggest arrangement of blooms I advertised on my website, three hundred dollars worth of flowers! He had told me to pick my favorite colors; he was calling from out of town and would not be able to come in and choose them himself. I had questioned the validity of the call, afraid I would make an arrangement and Orson Williams would cancel, leaving me stuck with something I would not be able to sell to someone else. I didn't voice these concerns to Norman, for he assured me Orson was completely trustworthy. Besides, Mr. Williams had offered a credit card number even though he wished to pay in cash. I had chosen to trust him but had been questioning my decision since then. Now, I finally felt better and took Norman's word about his friend.

19

We had a pleasant impromptu dinner, and I realized how it really had turned into a first date of sorts. We even found that in spite of so many obvious differences, we had a lot in common: we both loved dogs, sleeping late on weekends, and of all things, scary movies. Furthermore, we were both business people and believed in going above and beyond the call of duty for our customers. I was surprised to learn we were so similar.

"I'm not so bad, am I?" Norman asked, when we were out at our cars and ready to leave one another.

"You're very nice, Norman. Thank you for dinner," I said, and I meant it.

"Becka, that wasn't dinner! That was just a casual encounter. Let me take you on a real date on Friday night." The way he said it left no room for refusal, and I didn't want to say no anyway. But I remembered something as we hugged.

"Your friend Orson is coming to get his flowers at seven, then I'll need a little time to get ready." I would bring my clothes to the shop and prepare there, to save time. I was quite sure that by then, I'd be very anxious to see Norman again. In fact, I was already missing him as he got into his car.

"Let's shoot for eight, then," he said, then he waved and was gone.

As much as I loved my work, the week went too slowly as I waited to see Norman again on Friday. I was bursting at the seams to tell everyone about our newfound flirtation, but I kept it under wraps to everyone but Karen, for what if Norman wasn't all he was seemingly turning out to be? I would be terribly embarrassed to have to eat crow.

Friday arrived, the day busy with spring in full bloom and summer right around the corner. Karen went home at six o'clock. I was putting the finishing touches on a fabulous arrangement for Orson Williams, using flowers in shades of purples and pinks: chrysanthemums, gerbera daisies, dahlias and the usual roses and carnations. I must have lost track of time, because suddenly Norman was walking through the door in a blazer and tie. The arrangement was done, but I was confused: was it eight o'clock already? Had Orson Williams stood me up? Had I wasted my time after all on the expensive arrangement?

To my chagrin, I felt tears flooding my eyes. I was so puzzled: the clock read only seven, but here was Norman looking so handsome while I was still in my work clothes. He had a sneaky grin on his face that quickly turned to a look of concern when he saw how emotional I was.

"I thought we were going at eight. . .don't you remember? Orson is supposed to be here at—"

Norman reached for my hand and drew me into him. He smelled so strong, manly, virile. I felt like a big baby in his arms.

20

"Becka, I have a confession to make." Norman lifted my face to look up at him. "There is no Orson Williams. I made that name up so I could buy you the best bouquet of flowers you have. It's just beautiful, and it's for you, you made it for yourself."

What he said made me cry even harder, but they were tears of joy. Still, I managed to blurt, "You brat!"

He brushed his lips over mine, our first kiss, so light and sweet. "Go and get ready. Take your time. I'll wait as long as it takes." Norman sat down in a small waiting area I had set up and picked up a binder of arrangements. He began studying the pictures with great interest.

I rushed through getting ready anyway, because I couldn't wait for him to see me in my clingy red dress and heels, my long blond hair flowing nearly to my waist. When I walked back into the front of the shop, he immediately returned the binder to its table, staring at me as if spellbound.

"Becka, you are a bloom!" He exclaimed. And I felt like it too, as he gathered me into his strong arms and kissed me once again—the second kiss. "It's going to be a great night," he predicted.

He was right, for what could be better than a candlelight dinner and tender kissing and cuddling in an elegant Victorian house in Rolling Hills?

And it was only the beginning, for to everyone's surprise including my own, Norman and I became a couple. It took some time for my parents and friends to get used to the fact that Norman wasn't the man he used to be, but within a year they grew to love him as much as I did. Norman and I got married two years after we met and now live in his family home in Rolling Hills. So for me, living there turned out to be more than just a silly dream. Together, we have decided to wait to have children, but we want to have at least one and maybe adopt a baby too. For now, we are happily running our businesses and traveling to tropical paradises whenever we can get away. Life is good.

THE END

SOLE SURVIVOR
I Lost Three Sisters To Cancer

Pulling into the parking lot of the adult care home Mom had lived in for almost five years, I had no idea how to break the news to her. How could I be strong for my mother when my own heart was splintered into a million pieces?

My husband, Rick, offered to tell Mom himself, but I couldn't let him. My sister had just died and it was my responsibility to break the news to my mother. She had already lost two daughters to cancer and a husband to a broken heart. I worried how she would handle this most recent loss.

Mom had known Charlotte's health had been bad for the past couple of months, but she'd held out so much hope. Mom prayed constantly, believing God wouldn't have given her four daughters just to take them all from her.

"You know how your dad and I prayed to have babies for so many years," she'd told me just last week. And I did know. I'd heard the story many times growing up, and after each of my first two sisters' deaths. My parents had been married almost eleven years, praying every day for a baby. Finally, Charlotte was born, followed quickly by three more girls.

"God gave me four daughters." Mom cried as I held her hand the previous week and told her the doctors couldn't do any more for Charlotte. "He's taken two already, Abby." She sobbed. "He won't take another. He can't."

I'd held her while she cried, wanting so badly to believe her words. Wanting to believe a Mother's prayer could save her firstborn. But Mother's prayer hadn't been answered. Charlotte was dead and she'd suffered terribly for three days before she passed away.

When she died, I wasn't just sad, I was angry. Angry with God for ignoring my mother's prayers, angry with God for letting my sister suffer so much those last days of her life. I was angry because He'd taken all three of my sisters and left me to deal with their loss and my mother's grief. This was not the God of my childhood. The God my parents had taught me about was kind and good and loved me. That God didn't exist for me anymore.

My heart was heavy as I approached the doors of Clearwater Manor. Dried brown leaves swirled around my feet as I pulled open the door and stepped into the entry leading to the community living room.

Mom was in her usual chair in the corner, a book in her hand. She devoured books, reading three or four a week. She said they were an escape for her, helping her deal with her physical infirmities. I could only hope her books would help her escape from this loss as well.

Hearing the door close, Mom looked up from her book. Her eyes met mine and I could see the tears begin to form. She knew. I hadn't even said the words but she knew. As I went and knelt in front of her she was already sobbing, mourning the loss of her eldest daughter.

"Why?" She cried, clutching my shoulders. "Why did God take her from me, Abby? Why not me? I'm old. Charlotte's only fifty-one, she's still young and her girls need her." More tears came and all I could do was wrap my arms around her.

I'd been asking the same questions for the past two hours. I also wondered why He had taken her and not me. I almost felt guilty for being the only one left. And, naturally, I wondered when it would be my time. With three sisters dead from cancer, did I stand a chance of surviving to old age like my mother? Or would I suffer before dying as Charlotte had?

My knees were aching, so I stood and pulled another chair next to Mom's, holding her hand, rubbing her back for a long time, letting her cry, allowing her to vent her fury at the loss of another child.

The other residents, a few who were long-time friends of Mom's, came and offered their sympathy. Then we went to Mom's room to talk about the arrangements and to pick out the clothes she'd wear to the funeral.

Several times as we talked and went through her closet, Mom would break down and cry. I'd hold her, stifling my own emotions in order to be strong for her.

Only after we'd said good-bye and I was in my car did I finally release the pent-up emotions I'd held in during the visit. I put my head on the steering wheel, sobbing with grief and pain and so many other emotions I couldn't even identify.

Charlotte and I had been so close. After our sisters' deaths, I think we both felt if we held each other close, nothing could happen to us. But we were wrong. Now Charlotte was gone, too. I had no sisters left. There was no one to help me through, no one to help me comfort our mother.

This loss was the most difficult. I'd not only lost another sister, I'd lost the faith that had sustained me during the funerals of my other family members. I couldn't pray. I couldn't ask God to help me get through the days ahead. God hadn't heard my prayers to spare Charlotte's life. He hadn't heard my mother's prayers. Why bother praying?

Somehow, we got through the next three days. The visitation at the funeral home was torture. After several hours, it became impossible for me to hug another person. No matter what anyone thought, I had to get out of that funeral home. I had to be alone.

Rick caught up with me as I headed out the door. "Abby, where are you going?"

"I have to get out of here for a while, Rick."

"I'll go with you."

"No. Please, I need to be alone. I'll be all right. Take care of Mom."

He nodded, and I loved him more for understanding.

I went out to the parking lot and sat in our car for almost an hour. When my thoughts became more torturous than bearing all the grief of others, I went back inside. Mom looked at me with questioning eyes but didn't ask why I'd left. For that I was grateful.

The next day I again bore the horror of seeing another sister's casket suspended over a stark, cold hole in the earth. Charlotte would rest next to my other two sisters and our father. Her husband had given in to Mom's request to have her buried in our family's plot.

After the service, I selfishly hung back at the gravesite, asking my husband to take Mom to the car. I needed a moment to say good-bye before resuming my role as comforter to my mom. I looked past Charlotte's casket to the headstones beyond.

Memories of those three funerals raced through my head. The terrible aching sadness of losing the baby of the family overcame me even after all these years.

Janelle had been the light of Dad's life, a beautiful baby, a delightful little girl, and a pleasant teenager who grew into a lovely young woman—a woman who cared. Janelle devoted her life to helping abused children. She was a truly compassionate woman and had worked tirelessly for kids in our community through her position with the Children and Youth Services. We lost our sister when she died, but her kids, as she called them, lost a true advocate.

A few years later when Becky was diagnosed with cancer, it was more than Dad could take. We lost him to what we all believed was a broken heart. Not long after Dad's death, Becky was gone. She was only thirty-two years old and left her husband with two young sons. The boys eventually forgot the loving mother who'd nurtured them. That was painful to witness, though we knew it was only natural that their young minds would replace her with new memories. They were so little when they lost her. We continued to see the boys on holidays, even after Becky's husband remarried. And we did tell them about their mom—just a little, though, as their new mom was a good woman and we'd never want to upset her.

Fifteen years later I could still remember standing at the same plot, looking at Becky's casket. But back then I had a sister beside me.

Today I was the only sibling left. There was no sister to lean on, to talk to, to share my grief.

"Come on, babe." Rick was back, taking my arm. "It's cold. Come to the car."

I nodded, wiping the tears from my cheeks and the memories from my mind. Mom was waiting.

The funeral luncheon seemed to go on forever. I would've passed on the whole thing, but Mom had been adamant. "People come out for a funeral. You can't let them go away hungry, Abby."

At last, it was all over. We took Mom back to her place, and I held her again as she sobbed out her grief. When the tears subsided, she was exhausted. I helped her into bed and waited until she fell asleep before Rick and I headed home.

Rick was so good during that drive. He didn't talk, he didn't ask any questions. He just drove. Only when we were inside our home did he speak. He took my hand in his and tilted my chin up until I was looking into his eyes. "Abby, I can't begin to imagine how you truly feel inside. I still have my two brothers and sister and can't fathom how I'd deal with losing them one after another like you have. But I do know you, and I know you're strong enough to get through this. Your faith and your love of God will—"

"No!" I shouted, not allowing him to finish, pushing his hands away. "There is no God, Rick. How can I have faith when all of my sisters are dead? My eighty-six-year-old mother prayed to God to spare her daughter's life. Do you know how she prayed, Rick? She said, 'Dear Lord, you have two of my babies. Please don't take another. I need her here with me, Lord.'

"But Charlotte's gone, Rick. Mom's prayers weren't heard, and neither were mine. I can't pray anymore to a God that would turn away from a mother's pleading."

"Abby, please don't say that. We may not know the reason these things happen, but you can't give up. Your faith is what got you through the loss of your other sisters."

"That's what I thought, too, Rick. I thought God got me through those terrible times. But there's no reason for Charlotte's death. There's no reason my mother should have to go through this again. If there is a God, couldn't He have at least waited until after Mom was gone to take another of her daughters? Wasn't two enough?"

Rick took me in his arms. I gave in to the bottled up emotions inside and cried. I held onto my husband and sobbed until there were no tears left to shed. When I was completely drained, Rick lead me into the bedroom. Exhaustion took over. That night I slept in my clothes, waking in the morning with a horrible headache. The bed beside me was empty. Rick had gone to work without waking me.

I wanted to pull the covers up over my head and stay in bed all day, maybe even all week, but that wasn't possible. Our son would be heading back to college in a few hours. So I got up and made breakfast, allowed my son to hug me and comfort me, and then waved as he pulled out of the driveway.

After weeks of going back and forth between the hospital and my home, spending time with Charlotte and her family and Mom, then getting through seeing countless people at the funeral home and the cemetery and the luncheon, I was alone at last.

I shut off the radio that Ricky had left on, poured another cup of coffee, and sat at the kitchen table remembering.

My thoughts drifted back to happier times, to a childhood filled with wonderful memories. Loving parents who doted on their four daughters. Sisters who were always there for me. Family picnics, holidays, birthdays, all were cause for celebration because our parents were so grateful to have a family after so many years without children. We were always made aware of how long and hard they'd prayed for a baby and then were blessed by God with four daughters. Our home was always filled with laughter and prayer. We thanked God for each other as much as Mom and Dad thanked Him for us.

Then disaster struck for the first time. Our perfect, happy world was shattered when the baby of the family became ill. When the doctors finally found the cancerous growth, it had already sent tentacles around her organs, effectively shutting down her kidneys. Janelle lived for almost five months after her diagnosis. The world lost a very special young woman who was making a difference in the lives of children in need. She was practically a child herself; she was only twenty-four years old when she died.

We were all stunned by her death. We'd believed so fervently that our prayers would help heal her. Mom had been certain that God wouldn't take one of the daughters He'd blessed her with.

Yet even then, in the midst of our sorrow and pain, we turned to God and our faith to get us through. When Becky developed lung cancer, just three years after Janelle's death, that faith was tested again. It was too much for our dad. He died six months before Becky lost her battle with cancer.

Somehow, in the years following those two deaths, Charlotte and I drew strength from our mother's faith in God and from each other. As the years passed by and our children grew into young adults, we were happy again. We were a family, celebrating holidays and birthdays together as we had when we were young. And the sisterly bond between Charlotte and I grew stronger with each passing year. We truly were each other's best friends.

Five years ago, at eighty-one, Mom suffered a mild stroke that left her legs weak but her mind and voice and spirit intact. She could no longer keep her house, so my sister and I scoured all the personal care homes in our area, looking for a place where Mom would feel at home. We'd talked about her staying with one of us, but she wouldn't hear of it.

"You girls both have families and full-time jobs. It would be too much of an upheaval in your lives for you to have another woman living in your home."

She was right, of course. She would've been alone most of the day while we were at work. So we settled on a personal care home about a fifteen-minute drive from my house. I visited her quite often, even if it was just to stop and say hello on my way home from work. Charlotte visited often, too, and the grandkids when they were able.

Mom seemed content there as long as she had her stack of books to get her through the days and occasional sleepless nights. She still came to one of our homes for holidays and birthday celebrations. Although she got around the home fine with a walker, when she longed to go on a shopping trip, Charlotte and I would take to the mall using one of the shopping center's wheelchairs. We'd take her to any store she wanted to shop in. She loved being with her girls and called the wheelchair her own private chariot.

We'd gone through some tough times, but life was good again. Then one day, about two years ago, Charlotte came to see me. I could tell she'd been crying. "Is it Mom?" I asked, knowing she'd been to visit that morning. "Is something—"

She stopped me, shaking her head as tears streamed down her face. "No, no, Abby, it's not Mom. It's me. I found a lump in my breast." Her tears turned into great heaving sobs. I took her in my arms and held her, saying whatever I could to try and comfort her. "It'll be okay. It might not be malignant. Don't you give up."

She shook her head and blew her nose. "I already had the biopsy. I didn't want to tell you until I knew for sure. It's malignant. I'm scheduled for a mastectomy on Thursday."

I just stood there and stared at her. It was as though she was speaking another language and I didn't understand her words. "No," I finally murmured. "No. This can't be happening again. No." I shook my head as though that would make this awful news disappear.

Suddenly, I was crying and my big sister had me in her arms, comforting me.

When our tears subsided at last, we put the tea kettle on and sat down at the kitchen table. Our mom had always brewed a pot of tea when we had something on our minds, something that needed to be talked over. We carried on the tradition.

My sister reached across the table and took my hands in hers.

"Abby, will you be there for the girls if I don't make it?"

"Don't say that. Breast cancer is highly treatable. I know two women who've had the surgery and chemo and are still alive, one after five years, one going on three. You're going to be all right."

She smiled a faltering smile. "Okay. But just in case, will you be there for Megan and Cathy?"

"Of course," I said, knowing I had to reassure her even though I knew she wouldn't die. She couldn't die. I wouldn't allow her to.

I loved all four of my nieces and nephews, but Charlotte's two girls were special. We lived on the same street and her kids had been in our house almost as much as their own. We were all very close. I missed Megan when she went away to college almost as much as I missed my own son.

Cathy had just started high school the week before her mother's death. This was a difficult time for her. I couldn't imagine how the girls would cope with the next few years of their lives without their mom there to guide them.

Remembering the promise I made to my sister brought me back to the present. I needed to go and see her daughters. I couldn't even remember when Megan was leaving for college or if Cathy had gone back to school. I'd made my sister a promise yet had been so absorbed in my own grief that I'd forgotten to been there for her family.

I didn't call, just got ready and walked down the block to their house and rang the bell. John, Charlotte's husband, opened the door. He looked awful. I put my arms around him and felt his tears on my cheek, blending with my own. Then I felt other arms around me and turned to embrace Megan and Cathy.

"Aunt Abby, I'm so glad you came," Cathy said. "We didn't want to bother you but Megan hated to leave without saying good-bye."

"You're going back to school?" I asked.

Megan nodded. "I don't want to, but Dad thinks it would be best for us to get back to our classes."

"I'm sure he's right," I said, turning to John.

He nodded. "They've both missed so many classes these past few weeks."

His words drifted off and left me with images of all of us gathered around Charlotte's hospital bed. Twice we thought she was dying and she bounced back. Each time we believed it was prayer that had brought her through. But her final decline was horrific. She was in such awful pain; even the medication didn't help.

At one point I'd left her room and screamed silently at God: Enough! I couldn't understand why He would allow her to suffer so much. Where was the caring God we'd known for so long?

"Aunt Abby?"

Cathy's voice pulled me back from my thoughts. "I'm sorry, sweetie, what did you say?"

"I wondered if you could drive me to school tomorrow. I'm just not ready to get on the bus yet."

"Of course I will." I looked at the three of them, so exhausted, so emotionally drained. "I'll do whatever any of you need. I made a promise to my sister that I'd be there for all of you, and I'm just sorry I haven't been for the past few days."

John stood up and put his hands on my shoulders. "We know what you've gone through, Abby. We've lost Charlotte. You've lost the last of your three sisters. Our loss is great, but yours is tripled. If we can do anything to help you through, please know that we're here for you, too."

Tripled. The word stuck in my brain. Three sisters gone. Only memories now. I thought I had no tears left to shed but suddenly felt them trickling down my cheeks again.

Cathy and Megan came and put their arms around me. "We'll help each other, Aunt Abby. Somehow, with God's help, we'll get through this."

I shook my head, unwilling to depend on God anymore. "We'll get through it with each other's help," I said.

It looked like Cathy was about to say something, but Megan put a hand on her arm and shook her head. A look passed between them and I realized they must have heard me ranting about there being no God after their mother had been pronounced dead. I wanted to say something but knew it wasn't the right time. They still believed. I wouldn't take that away from them. I'd found comfort in my faith once. I'd let them have that now.

Days passed into weeks and weeks into another long month. The last of the autumn leaves were raked and bagged and only stark skeletal tree limbs remained. Winter was such a somber time, matching my mood.

I visited Mom more often since Charlotte was no longer there to share the visits. But each time, as I saw the pain in her eyes, it only increased my own.

Rick and our son, and even John and his girls, tried their best to pull me from my grief. "Please come to church with me, babe," Rick begged, but I refused. When Megan was home for a weekend, she'd call on Saturday night and ask if I'd go to church with them. I continued to turn down every invitation. I wasn't about to put my faith back in a God who'd deserted my mother and me.

Another month passed and the holiday season was upon us. Thanksgiving was a truly difficult day. We were all together at my house. Rick had picked Mom up for the day. But when it came time to say grace, I slipped back into the kitchen.

Megan called out, "Aunt Abby, we're waiting for you."

"Go ahead without me," I yelled back.

How could I give thanks when all my sisters were gone?

If I thought that holiday was bad, Christmas was awful. Every song on the radio reminded me of my loss. I never realized how many songs mentioned people going home for Christmas. When I was home alone, there was no radio or television on. It was simply too hard to see and hear about Christmas. The only reason we had a tree and a nativity set was because Rick and our son put them up.

Days continued to pass, and winter along with them. Suddenly, there was more sunshine and less snow. Eventually, crocuses began poking their heads through the thawing earth.

I didn't want spring to come. Winter, with all things dead and dried up, suited me because I, too, felt dead inside.

Rick caught me looking out the window at the flowers one day and put his arms around me. "Amazing how things come back again in the spring, isn't it?"

I didn't answer. I couldn't. Yes, the flowers were coming back, but Charlotte wasn't. She was gone and I'd never see her again.

"When you think about it," he continued, "it's a miracle each and every year. Trees that were barren all winter will soon have leaves again. And Easter's not far off. It's a real time of hope, Abby. A time that reassures us that God is watching over us and all is right with the world."

I didn't want to argue with him, so I just turned and walked away from the window.

Rick followed. "Abby, you can't go on like this. You have to allow God to help you heal."

I turned. "There is no God for me, Rick. If there ever was one, He deserted me when He allowed the last of my sisters to die."

"There is a God, Abby. You're angry with Him. That proves He exists. At least acknowledge that."

I shook my head and walked away, effectively stopping the conversation.

There was no stopping spring, though. Trees budded and daffodils poked their sunny yellow heads through the earth. Easter eggs appeared on trees in our neighbors' yards and crosses were visible in front of many churches, draped with purple cloth. Lent was a time of penance, a time of forgiveness. I still had none in my heart. I refused to forgive the One I felt was responsible for my sister's death. I was the only one who felt that way, though. Even my mother was back to praying.

One day during my visit with her, she said, "Abby, it's time."

"For what, Mom?"

"For you to talk to God again."

"Oh, Mom, let's not get into this, okay?"

She went on as though I hadn't spoken. "Rick talked to me and so did Cathy. They're worried about you, Abby. Your heart will never heal if you go on like this."

"I'll be fine, Mom."

Mom looked at me for several long seconds. "Are you having Easter dinner at your house?"

"Hadn't thought about it, but I guess I will."

"How can you celebrate a day that gives us all such hope if you don't believe in that hope?" she asked.

"I won't be celebrating, Mom. I'll be having dinner for my family." I turned and walked away, knowing I was hurting my mother but unable to talk anymore about hope and love and God.

On Easter morning I got up early to put the ham in the oven so it would be ready when everyone got back from church. Megan had already called the night before to ask me to go to church with them. I'd told her I'd be busy making dinner. She offered to help me that night and come in the morning so I could go to church. "Megan," I said firmly, "I'm not going."

Rick tried, too. He asked me to help straighten his tie and when I was finished, he put his arms around me. "Please go with me and Ricky," he said. "We'll sit with John and the girls."

I shook my head.

A few minutes later, my husband and son were gone and the house was silent. I sat down at the kitchen table, remembering the day my sister told me about her cancer. She'd taken my hands in hers right here at this table and asked me to be there for her girls.

I felt the tears coming and put my head in my hands. "I'm here for them, Charlotte," I whispered.

Are you? The question sounded like a whisper of spring air coming through the open door. My head jerked up as I stared at the doorway. No one was there.

But through the screen door I was able to see our church a block away. The cross in the front was no longer draped with a purple cloth. It was adorned with white lilies.

Even at this distance, though the words weren't clear, I knew the sign above it read, "He is risen."

"He is risen," I said aloud. I'd always believed those words, believed they were true. Because of that we, too, would have life after death. A thought suddenly slipped into my mind. God gave His only son. And God's own son had suffered a terrible death, as Charlotte had.

At that very moment I could almost hear my three sisters whisper, "Would you rather we were never born?"

I shook my head. My mother had prayed for babies and God answered her prayer. She would never have given up the joy of having

31

those babies, even if she'd known they would die before her. And I wouldn't have given up my years with them, either. It hurt so bad to lose them, but at least I had my memories of the times shared with each of them.

I could close my eyes and remember Charlotte and me waiting on the front porch for Daddy to bring our Mom and baby sister, Becky, home from the hospital. Charlotte and I did everything together, even back then. We were only a year apart in age, so it was almost like we were twins. We thought alike and sometimes finished each other's sentences. There were vivid memories of us playing with baby Janelle, too. She'd been an adorable little baby.

When first Janelle and then Becky died, Charlotte and I had held onto each other, our mother, and our faith. We'd grown closer with each of the deaths in our family, relying on each other for comfort and working together to help our Mom through her grief. The loss of our two sisters had given us an even stronger bond.

Through the years, as we raised our families, we continued to enjoy every minute of our time together. Our husbands often joked about it, though they never discouraged us from spending time with each other.

Charlotte and I shopped together, met for lunch or a movie. We rehashed books we'd both read and our families often had dinner together. We worked in my garden almost every spring, too. Charlotte—unlike me, who seemed to wither plants with a glance— had a green thumb. She'd planted every living thing surrounding our home. It was Charlotte who'd planted the daffodils that were blooming outside my door.

That's why I'd dreaded spring. That's why my heart ached so terribly. Spring had come, but Charlotte wasn't here to share it with me. I missed her so much and couldn't get past the fact that I'd never see her again.

Yet, Mom believed she'd see her girls again. She'd told me just last week that they were with their daddy, waiting for her.

At that very moment, with warm spring sunshine pouring through the doorway, I knew that I wanted to see them all again. Suddenly I knew I would. We'd all be together again one day. Cleansing tears came then, washing away all my doubts.

That Easter morning, my faith was renewed right there at my kitchen table. I could almost hear my sisters' voices saying, "See ya, sis."

For the first time in months a smile creased my face. If I hurried I could be with my family for the end of the Easter service.

Fifteen minutes later, I slipped into a pew next to my husband and son. Rick's smile started to melt the ice that had surrounded my heart for so long. Ricky reached past his dad and kissed my cheek. The choir was singing Alleluias as Megan, Cathy, and John all turned from their pew in front of us to hug me. The warmth of family continued the melting process.

Then I looked up at the image of the risen Christ above the altar, with angels on either side. As the choir sang, "He is risen . . . Alleluia," my voice joined the congregation's in the answering anthem. "He is risen indeed!"

THE END

IN LOVE WITH
THE EASTER BUNNY
What Can I Say? I Have A Weakness For Tails!

"Don't play with the ears, kid."

The voice coming out of the bunny suit sounded like it came from a gruff old man who'd spent too many years drinking and hanging out in dives where respectable rabbits wouldn't go, and it scared my daughter.

Alexis turned toward me and I could see the tears forming in her pale, blue eyes. I snatched her from the shopping mall Easter Bunny's lap and started to walk away.

"Hey, lady," said that irritating voice. "You didn't take a picture."

My daughter was sniffling into my shoulder when I turned back and said, "No, thank you. Not now. Not after you scared my daughter."

"You still gotta pay, picture or no picture."

"I'm sorry. I don't think so."

I turned again and had barely made it three steps when I felt the Easter Bunny's fuzzy, white paws clamp down on my shoulders. My daughter screamed.

I spun around and yelled, "Get your paws off of me!"

"I ain't lettin' go until you pay me my money."

The rank odor of alcohol and stale sweat oozed through the black mesh where the rabbit's mouth is. I wondered how many children had gotten a nose full of the aroma and how many of their parents would not have let their children sit on the Easter Bunny's lap if they knew.

I kicked the Easter Bunny in the shin, nearly losing my balance because I was wearing heels, had my purse and a full shopping bag hanging over one arm, and was still clutching my crying daughter to my chest. Then I kicked him again.

The photographer, a young woman in her teens, tried to step between us. The Easter Bunny pushed her aside and grabbed me again.

A couple of the children standing in line to see the Easter Bunny started crying, and one girl who didn't understand what was happening wailed, "Make her stop! She's hurting the Easter Bunny!"

By then the commotion had attracted the attention of mall security and two guards pulled us apart.

"She tried to leave without paying and then she assaulted me!" the Easter Bunny insisted.

The security guard restraining me appeared to be in his early thirties, only a few years older than me. The nametag on his chest read, Kensrue. He asked, "Is he telling the truth?"

"There's no way I'm going to pay him. He made my daughter cry."

"The Easter Bunny makes a lot of kids cry. It's even worse at Christmas. You'd be surprised how many kids cry when they sit on Santa's lap."

"If Santa smells like the guy in the bunny suit, it's no wonder."

My daughter had stopped screaming by then, but her cheeks were wet with tears. I dug in my purse for a tissue and wiped her face.

"What's your daughter's name?"

"Alexis."

He attracted Alexis's attention and asked, "Did the bunny scare you?"

My daughter nodded.

"Are you okay now?"

She sniffed, and then she nodded again.

"You and your mommy need to come to the office with me so we can get this straightened out."

"Okay."

"Why do we need to go to the office?" I asked.

"Do you really want to continue this conversation in front of all these people?"

I looked around and realized that we'd attracted quite a crowd, and I saw the other security guard holding the Easter Bunny's arm and telling him something I couldn't hear. I let Kensrue lead me away.

A few minutes later we were in an office behind a closed door and Alexis was sitting on the floor with a coloring book and some crayons that Kensrue had given her.

"So, what's in the shopping bag?" he asked. Kensrue sat behind a large, gray metal desk. The only thing on it was a yellow legal pad and a pencil.

"An Easter dress and new shoes for my daughter."

"Did you steal those, too?"

"I didn't steal anything."

"It's ten dollars to sit on the bunny's lap, picture or no picture."

"I'm not paying."

"Not paying the bunny is theft. It's like shoplifting."

I crossed my arms and stared at him.

"The bunny wants to file charges," the security guard said. "I don't think I can talk him out of it."

"Let him."

"That means a trip to the police station to be fingerprinted and have your picture taken," he explained. "Should I call your husband to come get your daughter?"

"I'm not married."

He looked at me. "Do you really want to put your daughter through all this?"

"The man in the bunny suit was rude and he smells like the restroom in a really low-class dive. He shouldn't be allowed near children."

"Maybe not," Kensrue said. "But I didn't hire him." He took a deep breath and continued, "He wants to file assault charges against you for kicking him."

"He grabbed me first. I should file charges against him."

"I'm certain I can prevent him from filing assault charges against you if you agree not to file charges against him."

"That's fine." I pushed my chair back and was about to stand. "Can I go?"

"Not yet. You still have to pay the ten dollars."

"No."

Kensrue doodled on the note pad for a moment. Then he asked, "Where are you taking Alexis that she needs a new Easter outfit?"

"Church. We always go to the sunrise service."

"Which church?"

I gave him the name.

"I have some friends who go there," Kensrue said. "They've invited me to join them half a dozen times. You might know them. The Worshams?"

Of course I know the Worshams. Kevin Worsham, a police sergeant, is a deacon; his wife, Maggie, leads one of the women's groups. "How do you know them?"

"Kevin and I work together."

It took me a moment to put the pieces together, but then I asked, "You're a cop?"

"I've been on the force ever since I graduated from the police academy. Mall security is just a part-time job."

"Your wife must be lonely if you're working all the time."

"I'm not married, not seeing anyone, don't even have any prospects," Kensrue explained. "The extra job fills up my spare time and I'm saving what I earn from this to use as a down payment on a house. What about you?"

"Me?"

"You said you're not married," Kensrue prompted.

"Divorced. When Alexis's father found out that I was pregnant and that I wouldn't—" I hesitated, because I don't often tell anyone what I was about to tell Kensrue and I had no idea why I was telling him. "—terminate the pregnancy, he filed for divorce. Our divorce was final two weeks after Alexis was born."

Alexis heard her name and stopped coloring. She looked up at me as if waiting for me to say more. I didn't.

Kensrue doodled on his pad without taking his eyes off of me. The only sound in the room was the point of his pencil marking the paper. He finally broke the near-silence. "Here's my dilemma. If this matter doesn't get resolved before we leave this room, I have to stop being a security guard and start being a cop. That means arresting you and everything that follows."

"Fingerprinting and photographs. You already told me."

He doodled a little more, and then pushed his chair back and stood. "I think I know how to resolve the problem. I'll return in a few minutes."

He left Alexis and me alone in the office. While Kensrue was gone, my daughter climbed into my lap and asked when we could go home.

"I'm not sure."

"This is because the Easter Bunny was bad, isn't it?"

I told her it was.

Before I could say anything else, Kensrue returned. "You're free to go."

"That's it?"

"Everything is taken care of," Kensrue said.

"Just like that?" I asked. I stood and grabbed my purse. "If this was so easy to resolve, why did you keep us here so long?"

Kensrue didn't answer my question. Instead, he handed me the shopping bag containing Alexis's new Easter outfit and then led us out of the mall's security office. He walked us to my car—perhaps to ensure that we didn't return to the rabbit hutch in the middle of the mall—and the last I saw of him that day was when he waved good-bye to Alexis.

I was surprised when she returned his wave.

Faith alone was insufficient to rouse me from bed two days later. On Easter morning I awoke long before sunrise, and then only because I turned my alarm clock to full volume and put it on the far side of my bedroom. I crawled from bed to silence the irritating, electronic caterwaul, and then showered before waking Alexis.

I dressed her in her new Easter outfit and I dressed in something appropriate that I'd purchased the previous Easter. Then I fixed our hair and did my makeup.

"I'm hungry," Alexis said just as we were headed out the door.

"We'll eat after sunrise service," I told her.

"I'm thirsty, too."

I stopped long enough to let her take a few sips of water, and then we drove to the park. We joined the rest of our congregation at the east end of the park, where it overlooked the lake and settled into two seats on the back row just as the first tendril of morning sunlight climbed into the sky behind our pastor.

He began the service by reminding the congregation why we celebrate Easter—an event that has nothing to do with men in bunny suits, gaily-colored eggs, or marshmallow chickens.

As Alexis and I prepared to leave I saw Kensrue, the shopping mall security guard, standing with the Kevin and Maggie Worsham. He wore an expensive, well-tailored gray suit over a crisp, white shirt and a dark blue tie. His black shoes were highly polished. He didn't look as imposing as he did in his uniform, but he's still a big man. I was so surprised that I stopped dead in my tracks.

Kensrue saw me and walked over to us. "I was hoping you'd be here."

I swallowed hard. "Why?"

"To give you this." He tried to hand me a coupon for a free photograph with the Easter Bunny, but I wouldn't take it.

"Don't worry," he said. "The man who was wearing the suit Friday won't be in it today. He was fired yesterday for drinking on the job."

I know I shouldn't have been snippy, but I couldn't stop myself. "Did they find another bum to wear the bunny suit?"

"I wouldn't say that. The mall staff didn't have time to hire someone, so I volunteered to wear the suit."

"You?"

"Today's the last day for photographs with the Easter Bunny," he continued. "I'll be in the suit from ten until four."

The Worshams joined us before I could respond. We greeted each other warmly, remarked on the beautiful sunrise, and discussed how appropriate the pastor's message had been.

Alexis tugged on my hand. When I looked down, she said, "I'm still hungry. You said we could eat after church."

"We will," I told her. "In a minute."

"The three of us were planning to breakfast at IHOP," Maggie Worsham told me. "We'd enjoy having you join us."

I glanced at Kensrue. The glimmer in his eye made me suspect that he and the Worshams had planned to invite us to breakfast and that Alexis's comment had simply made it easier for them.

"Pancakes!" Alexis squealed. "Can I get pancakes?"

"That's a yes, then?" Kensrue asked.

"That's a yes," I confirmed.

I learned two things at breakfast that day. Kensrue has a first name—Jonah—and that he gave the man in the bunny suit ten dollars out of his own pocket to make the problem at the mall disappear.

The photograph of Alexis sitting on the Easter Bunny's lap, wearing her Easter outfit and a grin that nearly split her face in two, is framed and hanging in our living room, right next to the wedding photo taken eight months later.

Those two photographs were the first things Jonah and I hung on the wall of our new home, a new home we never could have purchased if he hadn't saved all the money he'd earned working a second job as a security guard at the mall.

Lucky for our family, he no longer has to work a second job. Lucky for Alexis and me, Jonah was working the day I fought with the Easter Bunny.

THE END

I WENT EASTER EGG HUNTING–
AND FOUND SOMEBUNNY
WONDERFUL

My seven-year-old daughter, Sienna, and I walked beneath the huge, bare-limbed maples toward the admission gate of the charity Easter egg hunt. It was for a good cause—juvenile diabetes. A chilly breeze whipped Sienna's curls back from her face and penetrated my light jacket.

Proudly carrying her big, wheat-colored basket, Sienna didn't seem upset that it was the same one she had last year, just redecorated with new, lavender ribbons. We'd had fun sprucing it up the night before, along with baking Easter cookies and dying eggs.

"Hey, Maddie," a masculine voice said. Squinting against the bright sunlight, I glanced to my left and found Troy DiPalma with his daughter, Cassandra, heading in the same direction.

"Hi, Troy." I couldn't believe he even remembered my name. He was one of the popular kids in high school and never talked to me. My best friend was the one with a crush on him. I'd never aspired to date a guy who was the captain of the football team and the class president—well, maybe I had, in my wildest fantasies. He was also one of the cutest guys in school. If anything, he's even better looking now.

"Hi, Cassandra." I smiled at the little girl beside him, but she was glaring at Sienna. I glanced at my daughter and found her looking more uncertain than I'd seen her look in a while.

"Hello." Cassandra quickly strode to the entrance gate, paid her fee, and went inside.

"Sorry. She's in a bad mood today," Troy murmured with a sheepish but amused expression.

"No problem."

Troy jogged away and caught up with his daughter.

I stopped Sienna. "What's up with you and Cassandra?"

Sienna shrugged and grimaced. "She's a snob and majorly stuck on herself."

"Is she rude to you?"

"Sometimes. I just ignore her."

I knew exactly how Sienna felt because I felt the same way about Troy when I was in school. I had very unruly, naturally curly hair and the other kids in school often teased me about it. One day Troy called me frizz-head in a snide tone and then laughed with his friends.

I know I should've gotten over my petty, teenage angst, but when people rip away at your self-confidence it's hard to forget. Sienna has the same curly hair and I worry about the kids teasing her. Thank goodness hair care products have improved, so that I can always take special care in taming her curls.

A clattering noise behind us drew our attention. A huge, white Easter bunny drove a donkey cart in our direction.

Sienna's eyes lit up and she giggled. "Look at him, Mom! I wish Natalie could've come, but she had to go to her grandma's."

"You'll have to tell her all about the Easter bunny."

"Yep! And I want to have my picture taken with him."

Easter Bunny, dressed in a pink shirt and pastel green overalls, climbed down from the cart and patted the donkey. His assistant, dressed as a fuzzy, yellow chick held the donkey's reins as kids came over to pet him and shake Easter Bunny's hand. Only Sienna hung back shyly.

"Do you want to go over?"

She shrugged and crept forward hesitantly, but before she reached Easter Bunny, several kids, including Cassandra, led him toward the egg hunting area.

Sienna petted the donkey after the other kids ran to the starting line.

Easter Bunny did a countdown as Sienna and I paid our admission and rushed through the gate. The giant rabbit blew his trumpet and children scattered in all directions.

"Do you need help?" I asked Sienna.

After glancing around, she shook her head and ran toward a big clump of dry pampas grass. She pulled an orange and blue egg out, and then searched among the daffodils and tulips.

Troy sidled up to me. "They're cute, aren't they?"

"Sure are." I smiled and tried not to let Troy and his masculine appeals distract me from watching the kids.

I noticed Cassandra running around like a chicken, swinging her empty basket this way and that. Her pink, plastic grass fell out and she had to retrieve it several times. Maybe she needed help, but I wasn't going to tell Troy that.

"You work over at the bank, don't you?" he asked.

"Yep, I'm a teller." I knew he didn't have an account at Rosedale Savings.

"I have an aunt who works there. Wanda."

"You're kidding. I didn't know she was your aunt."

He nodded.

"And what about you? Still teaching at the college?"

"Yeah. Phys Ed, plus I coach football." Troy's eyes twinkled in the sunlight.

That was the longest I'd ever spoken to him. I was mystified he'd even speak to me at all. I wondered if he still had the abs he had years ago. Probably not. I glanced at his midsection but couldn't tell with his pale blue polo shirt.

"Man! Cassandra isn't going to find any eggs if she doesn't slow down and concentrate," he muttered with a frown. "She's upset because her mom went on a cruise with her new boyfriend and left her with me."

I'd heard Troy was divorced, but I didn't want to bring up the subject. "That's too bad. Easter is a special time for kids."

He nodded. "I'm glad she's staying with me this week. We'll go to my parents' house on Sunday for a big dinner. I just wish she'd get over her mad spell and realize that Brandi and I are never getting back together."

"Kids do keep that fantasy." Sienna certainly did until my ex-husband remarried.

"You married Billy Tyler, didn't you?"

"Yeah, but we've been divorced for three years."

"It's hard on the kids, isn't it?"

"Definitely, but Sienna's handled it pretty well. She's shy, but I think that's just her nature." Shy like I used to be.

Sienna ran toward me. "Look, Mom!" She held up her basket and I noticed a glittery, gold egg on top of the other colored ones. "The prize egg," she said in a quiet tone. Her smile was wide and she did a little jump, her curls bouncing.

"Wow!"

"Hey, that's great." Troy gave Sienna a genuine smile.

"There are only two of them and the winners get bicycles."

"Really?" I asked, stunned.

She nodded, dashed toward a juniper, and pulled a hot-pink egg from beneath it.

"I had no idea the prizes were that good," I said.

"Me neither."

Troy and I chatted a while longer, then he excused himself to talk with a coworker.

A few minutes later I noticed Sienna was chasing Cassandra. Cassandra yelled something at her. Sienna turned away in tears, and then dashed toward me.

"What's going on?" I asked.

"Cassandra stole my prize egg!"

"You've got to be kidding."

"No. It's mine! Tell her dad to make her give it back!"

Oh, dear. Just perfect. A fight over an Easter egg. I felt extremely uncomfortable telling Troy that his daughter was an egg thief. Seemed kind of petty, but it was for a bicycle, after all. I was sure Cassandra already had a bicycle, considering both her parents obviously earned good incomes and drove new cars.

"Your bicycle is only a little over a year old, Sienna."

"I know. It's not for me! I'm going to give it to Natalie. She doesn't have a bicycle."

I knelt before her. "Really?"

"Yes. That way, we can both ride at the same time instead of taking turns on mine."

"You are so sweet." I kissed her forehead.

I rose and sucked in a deep breath. Those old insecurities tightened my stomach as I approached Troy and his coworker.

Troy paused and glanced at me. "Is something wrong?"

I nodded.

He excused himself and walked with me toward Sienna, where she stood with tears streaming down her cheeks.

"What happened? Is she hurt?" he asked with concern.

"It seems Cassandra has taken Sienna's prize egg." I held my breath and waited for his response, half-expecting him to deny such an accusation.

"She did?" He frowned.

Sienna nodded, fear in her tear-filled eyes.

"I'll be right back." He strode across the large lawn toward his daughter.

When he confronted her, Cassandra yelled in denial that she didn't take the egg, then blamed it on another boy who happened to have found the other prize egg.

Troy shook his head. "We're leaving right now, missy. Come here."

"No!" Cassandra ran away but Troy, being a coach and obviously in great shape himself, easily caught her. He lifted her, kicking and screaming, into his arms. She threw down her Easter basket and the eggs went flying. Troy retrieved the golden egg and brought it to us.

I felt horrible that Cassandra was so upset, but she really did need to learn not to take things from others. Troy knelt by Sienna, far enough away so Cassandra wouldn't strike her.

"Here's your egg back, Sienna. Now, Cassandra, apologize."

"No!" She hid her face against his chest and sobbed.

"Okay, then we're leaving." He stood. "I'm sorry, Maddie and Sienna, that Cassandra stole the prize egg. I'll talk to you later," he said to me, and then strode toward the parking lot.

"I think she's in big trouble, don't you?"

Sienna nodded and held the golden egg against her chest as if it were made of real gold.

Ten minutes later, a photographer took Sienna's picture with the

Easter bunny as she held up the prize egg. The egg hunt organizer then gave us a voucher for a bicycle we needed to pick up at a local department store.

Sienna insisted we had to go to the store immediately. She was so excited that I imagined she'd forgotten all about giving the bike to Natalie. At the store, she looked over each bike carefully and chose a pink one.

"Why the pink one?" I asked. "I thought lavender is your favorite color."

"Because pink is Natalie's favorite color."

I wanted to hug her, but I held back.

On Sunday, after Easter services, we went to my parents' house for a huge dinner of honey glazed ham, deviled eggs, home canned green beans, potato salad, scalloped corn casserole, biscuits, apple crisp, and strawberry pie, among other things. We had another Easter egg hunt for Sienna and her eight cousins.

That evening at home, Sienna watched out our front window for Natalie's parents to return from her grandma's.

"They're home! Let's take the bicycle to Natalie!" Sienna yanked on her jacket and rolled the bicycle toward the door.

At Natalie's house, I knocked on the broken storm door and tried not to look at the peeling, white paint of the weathered, wooden siding.

Natalie and her mom came to the door.

"Hey, Sienna!" Natalie said. "Did you get a new bicycle?"

"No, it's for you."

Natalie's eyes widened. "What do you mean? You bought me a bicycle?"

"No, we can't accept this," Natalie's mother said. "We don't take handouts."

"We didn't buy it. I won it at the Easter egg hunt and I want to give it to Natalie," Sienna told her mother.

"Really?" she asked me, her frown lifting.

I nodded. "It was totally her idea."

Natalie jumped up and down and hugged Sienna.

A few weeks later, I took Sienna to the public library and we saw Troy and Cassandra in the children's section.

From across the room, Troy waved to us and smiled. He then whispered something to his daughter.

Cassandra looked uncertain as she crept forward, holding a forgotten book in her hand. She stopped in front of Sienna. "I'm sorry I took your prize egg," she murmured, truly seeming contrite.

"It's okay. Are there any more Mostly Ghostly books left?" The two girls scurried toward the shelf.

Troy approached with a warm smile.

"That was very nice of Cassandra to apologize," I said.

"I got her into counseling. The divorce is harder on her than I realized and she was acting out everywhere. She's doing much better now."

"I'm glad. She's a sweet and beautiful little girl."

"Thanks. Sienna is, too. I heard that she gave the bicycle to a girl who didn't have one."

I nodded, pride and emotion swelling in my chest. "She amazes me with how compassionate and generous she is."

We stood in silence a couple minutes, during which time I tried to think of something intelligent to say. I failed miserably because I realized I was becoming more attracted to Troy, something I had no business doing. He'd always been out of my league and he still is. He wore expensive cologne and smelled heavenly.

"So . . . are you seeing anyone?" he asked in a low voice.

"What?" He couldn't mean what I thought he did.

He sent me a devastating grin. "Are you dating someone?"

My heart felt as if it skidded to a halt. "No. Why?"

"I was wondering if you would go out with me sometime?"

The walls of the library seemed to be shrinking in on me. "You're kidding."

"No, why would I be kidding?"

"Because you're Troy DiPalma and I'm . . . me." My face burned.

He laughed. "What's that supposed to mean?"

"Never mind. I'm sorry. Sienna and I need to get going." Feeling like an idiot, I strode away from him. He probably thought I had no social skills.

"Sienna, come on, honey. We're going to be late."

I noticed the perplexed expression on Troy's face as we left the library, but I didn't have the guts to tell him how I felt.

Three nights later, Troy called me at home.

"Maddie, I'm sorry to bother you, but I'm still concerned about our last conversation."

"I'm sorry." Mortification burned over me even as my heart rate sped up with excitement. "I just don't think it's a good idea for us to go out."

"Why not?"

I hated the pettiness I felt inside. The truth was, I didn't trust him or his intentions. I could just imagine him talking about me behind my back with his professor friends, laughing at my poor way of life, my cheap clothing, and my twelve-year-old car with its rusty spots.

"Did I say or do something to offend you?" he asked.

"Not recently," I said, and then regretted it.

"Recently? Have I ever done something to offend you? If I have, please let me know."

45

I didn't want to tell him anything, but I knew he wouldn't leave it alone. Besides, maybe it would help me if I got it off my chest. "When we were in high school, you and your friends did . . . ridicule me a few times."

"I'm sorry, Maddie." His deep voice dropped. "I was such a jerk in high school."

You're right about that, I wanted to say, but didn't.

"Please accept my apology and let me make it up to you. I'd love it if you'd go out to dinner with me."

I wanted to say no, but he honestly did seem nicer now. Maybe he had changed. And I couldn't fight my growing attraction for him. Though I kept thinking I'd regret it, I agreed to go out to dinner with Troy.

He took me to an expensive restaurant. He's just trying to impress me, I figured, then stared in horror at all the silverware. I never can remember which fork goes with which course.

"You look beautiful tonight," Troy said, gazing at me through the candlelight. His gorgeous eyes seemed sincere and interested, but I couldn't help wondering what he was truly thinking.

"Thank you."

"I love your hair."

My hair? I couldn't prevent the brittle, sarcastic laugh that escaped my mouth.

"What?" He frowned.

I shook my head and wished I could escape this ritzy cage. Instead, I took a deep breath. "My hair is what you used to tease me about."

"I did?" His eyes held a troubled expression. "Man, I must've been an idiot. Your hair is gorgeous."

"You don't remember how I looked in high school, do you?"

"Yes. You were pretty then, too, but I was too blind to see it."

I sent him a tight smile and sipped my water.

"You don't believe me?" he asked. "What will it take to convince you?"

"I don't know." I was wishing the night were over. I didn't like his intense scrutiny.

"You hate me," he said, point blank as if he'd just solved a problem.

I snorted. "I do not hate you, Troy."

"You won't forgive me. You think I'm the same insensitive jerk I was in high school."

"I don't know you well enough to say at this point."

"Aha. Well, you should give me a chance to prove myself. I deserve a chance, don't I?" A hint of a grin softened his mouth.

"Yes."

"Can we just forget about high school and start over now, as adults?

I know I'm a very different person now than I was then. I imagine you are, too."

I nodded. True, I was different. I had more self-confidence now, not that I was loaded with it, but I had more than I did at age seventeen. And from all appearances, Troy was telling the truth. He did seem like a different, more considerate person.

"Hi, I'm Troy DiPalma." He smiled and extended his hand across the table.

I laughed and shook his hand. "I'm Maddie Tyler. Nice to meet you."

I gave Troy the chance he asked for and each time we went out, I found myself trusting and liking him more than the last time.

The first time he kissed me, on our second date, I felt his sincerity along with the incredible chemistry that simmered between us. That was when I knew he actually liked me. Me, Maddie Palmer Tyler. And he wasn't going to go talk about me to his friends and laugh at my gullibility. His kisses were gentle, affectionate, and attentive. He made me feel desirable again.

One night, we went to the movies and were surprised to run into his ex-wife and daughter in the lobby.

Brandi, who is perfect trophy wife material, scowled when she first saw me, but then tried to cover it with a fake smile. She'd also gone to the same high school as Troy and I. Back then she was, of course, a cheerleader and head of the popular clique.

"Troy, I didn't know you were dating someone."

"Yes. You remember Maddie."

"How are you?" The fake smile appeared again.

"Why didn't you go to the movies with us, Daddy?" Cassandra demanded in a shrill voice.

"I didn't know you were coming."

"Why are you here with Sienna's mom?"

"I'll explain it to you later, sweetheart."

"No!" Cassandra tossed her drink at Troy's feet and ran, crying, into the bathroom.

Brandi muttered a curse and glared at us. "Thanks for ruining our evening, Troy." She followed Cassandra.

"Jeez. Just great." He tried to kick some of the soda from his leather loafers as a theater employee came over and cleaned up the mess.

"We don't have to see a movie tonight if you don't want to," I said.

"I really thought she was improving."

"It's because of me. She sees me as a threat."

"But she doesn't treat Brandi's boyfriend this way."

"Did she at first?"

47

"I don't know." He threw up his hands.

Our date was cut short that night, but Troy patched things up with Cassandra over the next few days. Two weeks later Troy and I took Cassandra and Sienna to the zoo. They got along wonderfully, thank goodness, and Cassandra didn't throw any tantrums.

Troy and I have been dating six months. We're taking it slow, getting to know one another and each other's kids. I know I'm in love with him, but I haven't told him yet. Maybe one day, when we're all ready, our relationship will move to the next level. But right now, I have to say I'm happier than I've been in years and I hope things only get better. I'll always think of Troy as my Easter prize.

THE END

EASTER MAGIC
Hopping Into His Heart

The bunny suit did not flatter my figure in any way. The fluffy, white tail made my behind look big. The oversized rabbit head with the idiotic grin permanently painted on its face made it difficult for me to look down to see where my floppy bunny feet were going without pitching face-first to the floor.

My sister had an overloaded Easter basket in one hand. She pushed the bedroom door open.

"Are you ready yet? The kids are waiting."

My niece had the misfortune of having her sixth birthday fall on Easter Sunday, and her mother had talked me into wearing a bunny suit at the party.

I turned from the mirror.

"Sure," I said. "Why not?"

"What did you say?"

Apparently, the mesh under the bunny's nose that allowed me to see out and to breathe fresh air in muffled my voice. I shook my head and held out my left paw so my sister could guide me to the backyard. She hung the basket over my arm and then took my paw.

As soon as we stepped through the back door, the children crowded around me—all except for a little boy who ran away screaming and wrapped his arms around the legs of a handsome man standing with the other adults. Olivia had to shoo everyone away so that I could get down the stairs safely.

When I had my big bunny feet firmly planted on the lawn, I started handing out candy from the basket. My bunny paws were unwieldy, so I spilled nearly as much candy as I passed out. My sister walked behind me, replacing the spilled candy as we moved across the yard.

I spent half an hour with the children and then, with my sister's help, returned to the house. I was only too happy to shed the suit the moment she closed the bedroom door behind me. I stepped into the master bathroom; pulled on the clothes I'd been wearing earlier, and adjusted the scrunchie holding my ponytail in place.

After I stuffed the bunny suit in the shower and pulled the curtain closed so no one would see it by accident, and when I felt certain I didn't look any worse for wear, I returned to the backyard.

My niece ran up to me, put one hand on her hip, and demanded in her most adult six-year-old voice, "Aunt Elyse, where were you?"

"I was inside." I squatted down so that I was eye-level with Jacklyn. "Why?"

"The Easter Bunny was here and you missed him."

"He was?" I popped up and looked all around. "Where is he now?"

"He left."

I turned to my brother-in-law, Jason.

"Was the Easter Bunny really here?"

"Yep, he was."

I returned my attention to my niece.

"I'm sorry I missed him."

"Here." She handed me a peanut butter-filled chocolate egg. "He left this for you."

I took it from her hand and thanked her. She returned to her friends while I unwrapped and ate the chocolate egg.

"Nice tail."

I turned to find the handsome man I last saw with a little boy wrapped around his legs.

"Excuse me?"

"On the rabbit," he said. "Big and fluffy."

"So, you had your eye on the rabbit's tail, did you?"

He smiled.

"The Easter Bunny sure frightened your son."

"Nephew," he corrected. "My sister had to work today and she asked me to bring him."

"No children of your own?"

He shook his head.

"Matt's enough for me. His dad was killed in Iraq six months after he was born, so I've been helping my sister raise him ever since."

"How do you know Jacklyn?"

"The kids attend the same kindergarten."

Olivia interrupted us.

"Help me with the cake."

I excused myself and followed my sister into the kitchen. As she unboxed the bunny-shaped carrot cake and inserted six candles, she said, "I see you latched onto Dale, the only single man here."

"I didn't 'latch onto him,'" I protested. "He approached me."

Olivia looked at me over the top of her wire-frame glasses.

"Mm-hmmm."

"He said he liked my tail!"

"I'm sure he does," she said. "And why wouldn't he? You wiggled it at him."

"I did not!"

Olivia lit the candles and said, "Hold the door for me."

I pushed the screen door open and stood aside as she walked out with the cake. She carried it to the picnic table where all the children were sitting, placed it in front of her daughter, and told Jacklyn to make a wish.

My niece squeezed her eyes closed. A moment later they popped open. Then she took a deep breath and blew out all six candles.

Obviously pleased with herself, Jacklyn turned to her mother and said, "Know what I wished for?"

"It might not come true if you—" my sister started to say.

Jacklyn interrupted her. "A cousin. I want a cousin."

I glared at my sister. Her husband is an only child and I'm my sister's only sibling. If Jacklyn were to ever have a cousin, it would be up to me.

"What have you been telling her?"

Olivia threw up her hands in protest.

"I haven't said a thing."

Then she cut the cake, giving Jacklyn half of an ear, and slightly smaller pieces to the other children. Once all the children were served, my sister finished cutting the cake and had me offer slices to the adults sitting in lawn chairs on the far side of the yard.

I started with the mothers and ended with Dale. Then I settled onto an empty chair beside him.

"Your nephew seems to be doing better now."

"There's cake." He forked a piece of carrot cake into his mouth, as if to emphasize the point. "As long as there's cake, he'll be fine."

I smiled.

"So, you're Jacklyn's aunt?"

"Elyse," I said, introducing myself.

"Dale."

He stuck his fork in his cake and held out his free hand. I took it. He had a firm grip, but not too firm. A pleasant feeling of warmth spread through my entire body.

After reluctantly releasing Dale's hand, I asked, "What does your sister do that she has to work Easter Sunday?"

"Emergency Room nurse," he said, as we watched Jacklyn open her gifts. "She works nights and weekends."

"Finding reliable childcare must've been difficult for her. My sister had a hard enough time finding a good daycare center, and they work regular hours."

"I moved in with my sister so I can watch Matt," he explained. "It was just easier that way."

"What do you do when you're not watching your nephew?"

"Outside of work?" he said between bites of cake. "Not as much as I used to. These days I spend my evenings with Matt. The highlight of the day for both of us is when I read him his bedtime story. What about you? What do you do when you're not hopping around in a bunny suit?"

"Librarian," I told him.

"Really? Which branch?"

Before I could respond, Dale's nephew swung his arm around, caught a pitcher of raspberry-flavored drink, and poured it all over himself.

Dale leapt out of his chair and rushed across the backyard. I wasn't far behind. By the time we reached his nephew, my sister was already sopping the raspberry drink off Matt with paper towels.

"That's going to stain if we don't do something about it," my sister said.

Dale scooped his nephew into his arms.

"Come on, champ. Let's go home and get you out of these wet clothes," he said. "Say good-bye to Jacklyn."

Matt waved to my niece.

"Happy birfday."

And then they were gone.

The party didn't last much longer. Parents who'd dropped off their children arrived to retrieve them, and the mothers who'd stayed for the party also gathered up their kids and headed out.

I helped my sister clean up after the last child left. We let Jacklyn play with her new toys in the backyard while Jason carried all the trash to the can on the side of the garage. Olivia and I carried the dirty dishes into the kitchen.

My sister had just started washing them when I asked, "Why did Jacklyn wish for a cousin?"

"How should I know?" my sister replied.

"It was me," my brother-in-law said.

Jason came from the front of the house and we didn't hear him join us in the kitchen.

I turned to face him, a dishtowel in one hand and the cake server in the other.

"And what did you tell her?"

"She told me she wanted a little brother, and I told her that wasn't possible."

My sister was lucky to have Jacklyn. She isn't able to have additional children.

"Then I told her she might have a little cousin someday," Jason continued. "She didn't know what a cousin was, so I had to explain."

"When did you tell her all of this?" my sister asked.

She continued washing dishes and stacking them up in the dish drainer.

"Two or three weeks ago. I'm surprised she remembered."

"You're not the only one who was surprised," I said. "I'm the only person who can give Jacklyn what she wished for and I'm not married. I'm not even seeing anybody!"

"Are you going to dry that or wait until it dries itself?" my sister asked.

I quickly dried the cake server, placed it on the counter, and pulled a bowl from the drainer.

"I saw you talking to Dale," Jason said. "He's a nice guy, does a lot for his nephew, and takes good care of his sister."

My sister starting tapping on the window above the sink, apparently trying to get her daughter's attention.

"You'd better get out there," she said over her shoulder to her husband. "She's trying to dig a hole in the flowerbed using a fork we dropped."

Jason disappeared out the back door.

When she saw that he had taken the fork from their daughter and had brushed the dirt off Jacklyn, my sister returned her attention to me.

"He's right, you know."

"Who? About what?"

"Jason's right about Dale," she said. "He's a really nice guy."

We didn't talk about Dale again until Tuesday afternoon, when my sister called me at work.

As soon as I answered, she said, "I hope you don't mind, but Jason gave Dale your number."

"He did?" I asked. "Why?"

"Dale asked for it."

"When?"

"At lunch," she explained. "They work in the same building and apparently go to lunch at some of the same places. They happened to cross paths at the sandwich shop at the end of the block. They got to talking about you, and then Dale asked Jason if he thought it would be okay to call you. You know Jason. He didn't even think twice before giving Dale your number."

My brother-in-law has been trying to play matchmaker for me ever since marrying my sister, and his success rate was abysmal. I let him set me up on two blind dates before I realized that his idea of a good guy and my idea of one are polar opposites. That time, though, I didn't mind that he'd shared my phone number. I was actually glad he did.

Dale called that evening and reminded me who he is and how we'd met, as if he thought I could've forgotten him so quickly.

"Of course I remember who you are."

I heard Matt in the background, so I asked about him.

"He's no worse for having tried to drown himself at the birthday party," Dale said. "And I got his clothes in the wash in time to prevent stains."

"Your sister must have appreciated that."

"You know, I don't even remember telling her about that part of the day," he said. "I had to tell her about the rabbit that frightened her son."

"You didn't."

He laughed. "Don't worry. I promise not to ever tell her it was you inside the suit."

We spoke for a few more minutes before Dale finally asked me out.

"My sister doesn't work on Friday. I was wondering if you'd want to have dinner."

"I'd like to, but. . . ."

"But?"

"But we've having a mystery writer at the library on Friday. He's reading from his latest novel and then doing a Q&A with the audience."

"That sounds like fun," Dale said.

"Really?" Most of the men I had dated would have chewed off their own arm to avoid having someone read aloud to them. "Would you like to meet me at the library for the reading? Then, afterward, maybe we can stop for dessert."

"That sounds great."

I told him which branch I worked at and what time the reading began, and we ended the conversation by saying how much we were looking forward to seeing each other again.

I took extra care with my apparel Friday. It wasn't because of the library's guest speaker, but for my date that evening. Selecting something that flattered my figure wasn't difficult, but I needed to ensure that I wore something Dale found more appealing than a bunny suit with an oversized head.

The day crawled past. I must have checked my hair and my makeup a dozen times during the day. I wasn't certain why I was so nervous—I'd been on plenty of dates, after all—but I began pacing at six o'clock, a full hour before the reading was to begin.

The guest speaker arrived early. Luckily for me, another librarian was his liaison. She ensured that his needs were met. I checked and doubled-checked the room where the reading would be held, ensured that all the chairs were in place, that the speaker's books were properly displayed at the back of the room, and that he had a pitcher of cold water on a small table next to the lectern.

With no sign of my date at a few minutes before seven, I walked to the front of the room and greeted everyone. I told them where to find the restrooms and that no photography or recording would be allowed, and I instructed them to turn off all cell phones and other electronic devices.

"Our guest will be joining us in a moment, so sit back and enjoy yourselves."

While I was speaking, Dale arrived and slipped into an empty seat in the back row. I joined him a moment later and settled into the seat next to him.

"Sorry I was late," he said. "An accident on the highway has everything tied up and I had to find an alternate route."

I patted his hand and told him I was glad he'd made it. Before I could say anything else, the other librarian led the guest speaker to the lectern and everyone applauded.

The writer turned out to be a good reader and an entertaining speaker. Not all of the authors we invite to the library are. Afterward, I suggested a restaurant three blocks from the library that had great desserts, and Dale and I talked about the speaker. We discovered that neither of us had ever read the man's books and that both of us intended to purchase his latest.

We discussed other things over dessert as well: nieces and nephews, sisters, and our jobs. Dale told me about working in human resources, and about some of the crazy things people do to make their resumes and job applications stand out.

"It isn't just pastel-colored paper and odd fonts," he said. "I've had resumes delivered with homemade cookies and inappropriate photographs. I even had one resume delivered by a guy in a gorilla suit who said he would 'go ape for the opportunity' to interview for the job."

We laughed about that and about some of his other stories. We finished our cake, had our coffee refilled, and compared notes on favorite authors, favorite movies, and favorite television shows. We had our coffee refilled a second time and kept talking.

The restaurant was slow that night, so our waitress didn't try to hustle us along. At least three hours passed before we gave up our table. Dale left a tip out of proportion to the size of the check, and he walked me to my car in the library's parking lot.

It was a bit forward and out-of-character for me on a first date, but I subtly let Dale know he could kiss me as soon as we reached my car. He took the hint and covered my lips with his.

When the kiss ended, he said, "I hope we can do this again soon."

We did the following Friday, and again the Friday after that. It soon became obvious to both of us that we'd become a couple.

I didn't meet Dale's sister, Andrea, until we'd been dating for several weeks. I arrived at their house one Sunday to pick up Dale and Matt for an afternoon at the park. As I approached the house, I heard music from inside. Someone was playing a piano.

When I rang the bell, the music stopped.

A moment later, Dale's sister opened the door wearing pale green scrubs and said, "You must be Elyse. Dale has told me so much about you," she said as she let me into the house.

I would've noticed the family resemblance even if I didn't already know that they're brother and sister.

"He's in the back getting Matt ready."

I saw an upright piano in the living room and asked, "Was that you I heard playing?"

"It's something I do to relieve stress," she said. "Working in the ER drives some people to drink. It drives me straight to the piano."

Dale and Matt stepped into the living room and Dale asked, "So, you two have already met?"

"Not officially," his sister said.

Dale took the opportunity to introduce us, and then the three of us talked for a few more minutes before Andrea left for work. We left the house a few minutes later and took Matt to a nearby park. He played with a group of children while Dale and I sat on a nearby bench.

"You're practically Matt's father," I remarked.

"He knows I'm not," Dale said. "Andrea and I have made sure he knows about his father."

"But you're the only adult male in his life," I continued. "What's going to happen when that changes?"

"Why would that change?"

"Someday you might find the woman of your dreams."

"I already have." He took my hand in his.

"And you'll get married and move out of your sister's house."

"I won't go far," he said. "I'll still be there for him."

I smiled and patted the back of Dale's hand. He's a good uncle.

Before long our weekly dates became twice-weekly dates, and soon after that Dale and I were spending three and four evenings together. Most of the time we had Matt with us, and sometimes we included my niece so that Matt wouldn't be stuck with just grownups all the time.

Most evenings we were together we just hung out at Andrea's home, watching television and watching Matt. Occasionally we spent the evening with my sister and brother-in-law and the two children, but the only time Dale spent at my apartment was on Friday evenings when we could be alone.

One evening, after we'd been dating seriously for about five months, our physical relationship seemed like it was about to progress. Dale resisted.

"I can't."

"Can't?"

"I thought I could, but—"

"Is there something wrong with me?"

Startled, he said, "No. Not a thing. You're beautiful and I want you, but not like this. I was a bit of a player when I was younger. I thought that was okay, but after I moved in with my sister and started caring for Matt, I realized that's not the man I want to be. The next woman I make love to will be my wife."

How could I argue with that?

A week later Dale dropped to one knee and proposed. We married nine months after we first met at my niece's Easter birthday party.

We had a small wedding, with only immediate family in attendance. Jacklyn was the flower girl and Matt was the ring bearer. My sister was matron-of-honor and my brother-in-law was Dale's best man. Andrea provided the music, playing the Wedding March and two other songs on the church's piano. Our reception was dinner at a steakhouse with our little wedding party.

Dale and I had pooled our savings and used the money we didn't spend on a fancy wedding and reception for the down payment on a small, three-bedroom home in the same neighborhood as our sisters.

We chose the location of our new home for convenience. My sister lives five blocks in one direction and Dale's sister lives three blocks in another. Because we continued to care for Matt five or more days a week, we let him help us decorate one of the smaller bedrooms. We were in the house more than two months when I realized we'd have to start working on the third bedroom, too.

Less three months after we'd married, we were back at my sister's house celebrating Jacklyn's birthday. Because her birthday fell on a weekday, my sister hosted a smaller party. Matt, Dale, and I were the only guests. Andrea was invited, but she had to work.

My sister placed the cake in front of her daughter, seven candles burning away, and told her to make a wish.

Before Jacklyn had a chance to scrunch her eyes closed, I squatted down beside her and asked, "Do you remember what you wished for last year?"

Jacklyn shook her head.

"You wished for a cousin."

"I did?"

"And you're going to get some soon."

At the edge of my vision I saw my sister's eyes open wide.

"You mean you're—?"

"Yes," I said as I looked up at her. "Three months. Twins." Then I returned my attention to Jacklyn. "So be real careful what you wish for."

"I want a pony."

I laughed.

"Thank goodness, because that's not something your aunt can do for you."

I straightened up and rejoined my husband on the other side of the table, took his hand in mine, and smiled.

Maybe that bunny suit flattered my figure better than I'd thought.

THE END

THE PERFECT EASTER PRESENT
…And It's Not Chocolate Eggs,
Marshmallow Peeps or Easter Lillies!

"Emily, there's a call for you."

Sheila tapped my shoulder as she delivered this news. I turned away from the candy counter to ask her who was on the line, but she'd already disappeared into the back room.

My heart leapt. I knew it was either my sister or my new boyfriend, and the probability of it being the latter caused a rush of exhilaration to pump right through to my fingertips. I hurried to finish packing the order so that I could get to the phone in due speed.

"Slow down a little, Emily," my customer cautioned. "I don't want any of those candies cracked now, you hear?"

Of all the dumb luck, I had to have Ms. "Fussy" Baxter standing in the way of the phone. There was no one free to dump the order on, either. The traffic in the candy store on that day before Easter was second only to that on Valentine's Day. There were six of us squished behind the L-shaped counter and each of us was at least three-deep in customers waiting for service. If it were Michael on the phone, the prospect of talking to him anytime soon grew dimmer and dimmer. More than likely, he'd get tired of waiting and hang up before I could sneak a moment away.

"Emily Matthews, are you paying attention?" Ms. Baxter snapped. "I said that I'd like two turtles, not a boxful."

I stared down at the white box and, indeed, I'd piled the round delicacies to fill half the container without realizing it. Plucking them out and tossing them haphazardly back into their proper bins, I then moved over to the vanilla creams and placed four of them neatly into the box.

"What else would you like, ma'am?"

"Hmm. . . ."

The fussy matron placed a gloved hand over her lips to pause and then brought her hand back down to rest on the glass sheltering the chocolates, pointing in the general direction of the fruit assortments. "I suppose three raspberry and three maple."

I quickly scooped up the raspberry creams and slapped them into the box before sliding down the counter to the maples.

"Wait! No, Emily!" Ms. Baxter called out. "Not the raspberry; the strawberry would be more spring-y, don't you think? And just two maples and one of those divine-looking white chocolate creams over there." She waved her hand toward the opposite side of the store.

I stifled a groan. By now, Michael was surely hanging up. No just fairness to be found in that little town. Didn't Ms. Fussy understand that my beau was waiting for me?

Sucking on my upper lip, my level of frustration rising faster than the barometer on an August noon, I replaced the raspberry with the strawberry creams, plucked out a maple, and skittered it across the counter to put in its proper place later. Then I quickly began worming past my coworkers to the opposite side of the store to fetch a white cream. Working my way through the mess of activity proved to be tougher than it appeared. The rich aromas of sugar and chocolate choked my senses. Bobbing and weaving, dodging elbows and sliding sideways past oversized fannies, I finally arrived at the treasure and snatched up one of those lovely white confections to round out Ms. Baxter's half-pound box.

As I whipped around to make my way back across the store, I nearly knocked the vase of lilies off the back counter near the register. The vibrant bouquet was a gift from Betsy's beau. They'd arrived earlier that morning and Betsy promptly chose a prominent place in the store to ensure that the flowers taunted the rest of us all day long. Not only was Betsy the boss's daughter, favored employee, and an all-out braggart, but she was also an amazing beauty and blessed with fortune unknown to common girls like me. Boys flocked to her side and each beau tried to outdo the last in presents and impressive gestures. I, on the other hand, felt fortunate just to have a boy who was willing to pay attention to me. A boy who might be waiting on the telephone line, and as the minutes clicked by, he might be less willing to pay me any mind in the future.

I snapped a lid on the box, stretched a red ribbon across the glossy, gold-inscribed top, and wriggled my way back to Ms. Baxter. Sliding the box across the counter and into her hands, I thanked her properly, then turned and fled to the back room as fast as I could get past the other girls taking orders.

Blinking to adjust my eyes in the dim light, I made my way over to the desk with the phone. My thigh connected with the candy station cart and a blast of pain seared through my flesh, bringing tears to my eyes. But not even that agony detoured my determination as I snatched up the receiver resting on the desktop and squelched back the pain.

"Hello?"

"Hey, Emily, glad I caught you." My sister's voice poured like rancid syrup through the line. "Mawmaw wants you to pick up a dozen of those Easter egg chocolates for tomorrow and I'd like a box to bring to John's, as well. Can you get them before you leave?"

"Yes." I sighed and my heart dashed to the floor. "I'll be sure to bring 'em along. I should be home around suppertime."

"Oh, good. Are y'all busy today?"

"Of course. What did you think, Fanny? It is the day before Easter, you know."

Fanny had little conception of life. Work was beneath her. Pursuing marriage and social circles reigned as her supreme objectives.

I rushed her off the phone and rushed back out to the front of the shop before I caught hell for staying in the back too long. My shift was nearly over and Michael had still failed to call. I wasn't sure what to make of his neglect or if I should be worried. The next day was Easter and I wouldn't see him but for a moment or two at church and then we would go to our respective homes to join our family feasts. My sister, being properly engaged, would have the fortune of joining her fiancé for dinner. I thought that Michael would want to spend some time with me that night before the Easter festivities drew us apart. Well, there was still an hour before closing and perhaps he'd call by then.

With heavy spirits, I walked back out into the bright chaos of the shop.

"Next? Who can I help next?"

Two minutes to closing and we were still knee-deep in customers, so much so that I didn't notice a uniformed man handing Sally a package over the counter until the corner of the package nicked my cheek as she swung it down toward me.

"Ouch!" I lifted my hand to my cheek and felt the thin line of a scratch already forming. Great. Whenever I did see Michael again, I'd have a wound and he'd hardly want a thing to do with me.

"It's for you!" Sally exclaimed, her eyes widening with excitement.

I stared down at the rectangular, brown package with a mix of curiosity and wonder. Indeed, my name was scrawled on the outside of the package along with the shop address, and a return address of Hampshire Floral, the local flower and gift shop.

"Open it!" Sally prodded.

"Excuse me, miss, but are you going to finish my order?" the customer I was tending to interrupted.

"Of course. I'm so sorry."

I whisked the mystery package to the back counter and promptly turned my attention toward filling the order in front of me. Four customers later, my mind was whirling with all the possibilities of what the box contained and whom it was from. Is it from Mama? Was it sent here by mistake? Could it be from Michael? Did he send me candy? Or flowers? No, too heavy to be flowers. Is it a music box? I could hardly stand the anticipation. Every chance I had, I stared at the package and tried to burn a hole through the wrapping with my gaze.

The shop slowly emptied and I thanked my lucky stars that I had only one customer left in front of me. I filled that last box of candy so fast that I think that I broke any prior record established for the quickest candy order filler in the county and just maybe, in the whole state of Tennessee, too.

Sally appeared by my shoulder as I carefully picked up the neatly wrapped package from the counter. "Are you going to open it now?"

"Of course!"

We tittered in a nervous frenzy as we fled to the back room to indulge our curiosity in the contents.

As tempted as I was to tease Sally and open the package slowly, I dove into it like a cat clawing at a catnip toy. The heavy, brown wrapper gave way to a plain, cardboard box. I lifted the lid and peered inside.

There are moments in your life that you remember as clearly as the day you were born and there are moments that you will never forget as long as the sun rises. Surely, this was one of those sun-rising moments for me.

Sally and I stared at each other with a strange puzzlement brewing in the air between us as I slowly lifted the leather-bound book from its encasement. A white note card fluttered to the ground and I stooped to pick it up. Little, neatly typed letters inscribed the simple words: Emily, Happy Easter. Love, Michael on the face of the card.

Bewilderment isn't nearly a strong enough term for the flood of confusion that churned through me, but bewildered by that odd gift I was.

"He sent you a Bible?" Sally raised an eyebrow and reached out to touch the leather binding as if to certify that it was real.

A tear of humiliation slid down my cheek and much to my chagrin, a chorus of high-pitched laughter broke out behind me. I turned around to find Betsy and her best friend, Lori, standing there sharing their mirth at my expense.

"Oh, how sweet," Betsy said, drawing out the "sweet" in nails-across-chalkboard fashion.

A boy who admires you may send you a card. A boy who adores you may send you chocolates. A boy who worships the very ground you walk upon may send you expensive arrangements of Easter lilies. But what on earth does it mean when a boy sent you a Bible? That you're prudent, pure, God-fearing, and chaste—all the things I aspired to be, but not the qualities you care to have your high school sweetheart emphasize.

I held my chin up and wiped the speck of tears away from my cheek with the back of my hand. "Yes, it was sweet of Michael."

Betsy and Lori ignored me, resumed their condescending laughter, and skipped back to the front of the shop. They'd gotten their dig in and I wasn't worthy of another second of their precious time.

"Oh, Emily." Sally came over and patted my shoulder in a comforting manner. "Don't pay those two any mind. They have less sense than God gifted a cow. I'm sure that Michael meant well. After all, he is a rather shy boy."

"Shy" is the polite, southern way of saying "awkward and gangly." I knew that Michael wasn't the pick of the litter, but I'd grown rather fond of him, nonetheless. He'd proved to be the kindest, gentlest boy I'd ever known, and though I wouldn't dare to speak it aloud, he is an awfully fine kisser. So he didn't send me a romantic gift, but he still cared enough to send one and I would care enough to carry it proudly in my hands at Easter mass tomorrow. The notion brought some comfort, though my heart still longed for that brilliant lily bouquet.

Preparation for Easter service began at the crack of dawn as we women scurried around, pressing dresses and ties, buffing the last scuffs off our Sunday shoes, pinning curls, and dusting powder. Two hours later, my family arrived in fashion on the steps of Divinity Church to smile and greet our neighbors with warm holiday hellos. Several of Mama's friends commented on my fancy new Bible with its embossed leather jacket. As I explained where I'd gotten it, they nodded and signified their approval. Though he hadn't managed to impress my coworkers or me, Michael had certainly stumbled upon a way to gain favor with our elders.

We stood outside chatting for a moment under the warm sun, the scents of lilac perfume and freshly scrubbed linens intense around us. Michael and his parents arrived and he immediately made his way through the crowd to my side.

"Do you think your mama would object to my sitting with you today?"

"No, that would be right fine."

I blushed a little and drew the Bible up to my chest. I hadn't seen Michael the night before, as he was busy helping his daddy, and I only had the opportunity to offer a small thank you to him over the phone. I hoped that showing off his present would evoke a little more understanding of my appreciation for his plain, but thoughtful, gift.

Michael just kept on smiling and nodding with a funny glow about him like he'd just won a blue ribbon at the county fair. After a moment or two, the church bell rang and we all scurried to find our places inside before the service began. Michael slid into the pew beside me and Mama nodded to him as Papa shook his hand and offered a cordial Easter greeting. They both seemed pleased to have Michael accompany me.

All through the service, my heart leapt and fumbled, tripping over whether I was truly happy being Michael's girl or not, and whether or not he was truly happy with me. Trying to decipher why he'd chosen the quizzical gift perplexed me enough so that I missed most of the sermon and received several nudges from Mama when I neglected to stand or sit on cue.

Right before the Doxology, I placed the Bible beside me in order to grab a hymnal and my thumb caught the front cover of it. The leather sleeve lifted up to reveal an inscription on the inside cover. I never even thought to look for a note. I gently picked the Bible up and glanced at the wide, looped letters that clearly identified Michael's handwriting.

Dearest Emily,

I thought to give you flowers, candy, or other pretty baubles for Easter, but I knew my intentions go so much deeper than trinkets and ordinary gifts. I love you, Emily. I want to ask for your hand in marriage and I could think of no greater way to profess my love for you than to give you the greatest gift of love ever, written by God's own hand. If you are carrying this Bible with you at church on the morrow, I shall know that you feel the same.

With all my heart,

Michael.

In the sweep of the moment I was engaged, and as the tears welled up, I turned to look into the eyes of the most passionate man I've ever known. A man who realized that lasting relationships are not built upon passing fancies or pretty things, but are built upon solid faith, wisdom, and a lot of help from God.

I never looked at Michael in quite the same way again. A year later we were married and fifty years later, I still hold that leather-bound Bible. The pages are tattered and the leather is cracked, but it accompanies us to church each Sunday and rests upon our nightstand in between services, reminding me each morning and night of the love I so gratefully came to understand and cherish on that Easter Sunday so many years ago

It outshines every lily ever grown.

THE END

ONE EASTER MORNING
I Hunted For Eggs, But Found True Love!

"Go ahead, Mommy! You take the flower beds and look there!" my daughter called.

Immediately I spotted a bright, pinstriped egg lying in my tulip bed and a blue one nestled in the branches of a camellia bush.

I was utterly surprised by my children's eager insistence that I help them hunt for Easter eggs.

The past few years had been rough for them after their father died. I'd tried my hardest to maintain all the usual holiday traditions, but because my husband had died on Easter, we had difficulty re-creating the excitement of egg hunts.

My grandma always told me that true love burned the brightest, but that the brightest flames left the deepest scars. She probably spoke from experience because she and Grandpa were married for over fifty years and were as in love on the day he died as they were on the day they got married.

I had the same sort of bright burning love, but unlike Grandma's, the flame on my love was extinguished too early.

I'd met Peter when we were juniors in college and my theory about love at first sight—that it did not exist—was blown out of the water. Peter was the kindest soul I'd ever met. He wasn't drop-dead gorgeous and neither was I, for that matter. My dating experience prior to Peter was spotty, since my average looks were also accompanied by very low self-esteem.

Peter saw through my fears and dug straight through to my heart. I knew after that first date that I wanted to spend my life with this auburn-headed man who had freckles sprinkled across his nose.

"Liz, you know your kids will probably have frizzy, red hair with freckles head to toe, don't you?" My roommate, Julie, tended to look at a person only on the outside, as evidenced by the trail of tall, dark, and hunky football players in her wake. "When you combine your strawberry-blond hair with his, it's going to be a genetic disaster. It's just as easy to fall in love with a good-looking man as it is to fall in love with Carrot Top."

We'd had this discussion before, but it usually involved Julie's love du jour and how well his physical traits would mix with hers. "I don't care if we have kids with purple hair—and who says we're going to have kids, anyway?" I released an exasperated sigh. "We've only had three dates and. . . ."

"Yeah, but I see a starry look in your eyes and I've never seen it before. This guy must be the one," she said. "Or at least you think he's the one. Please, please, please consider the biological consequences, Liz. You should marry a dark-headed man so you'll have attractive children. That's why I only date guys with dark brown hair."

I shook my head and returned to my studies. Love at first sight or not, I had a psychology midterm the next day and I wanted to ace it.

And ace it I did. To celebrate I treated myself to pizza and a few chapters of a novel at the student union. As I lost myself in the international adventures of a world-renown spy, I didn't notice Peter enter and make his way to my table.

"Is that the one where the serial killer sends his victims gifts before he kidnaps them?"

Startled, I dropped my slice of pizza and it slithered off the table and dropped to the vinyl floor.

"Sorry," he said apologetically. "I didn't mean to scare you. I just thought I'd. . . ." His voice faded as a blush crept up his neck, accentuating his pale complexion and the hair color Julie was so dead set against.

"No worries. It's just pizza and they have plenty." I waved toward the food court pizza shop and reached for my purse.

"My treat, since it was my fault."

Peter ordered another slice of everything-but-anchovies pizza and slid the steaming food onto the table in front of me. "My apologies again. And I'll let you get back to your book." He spun and walked away, heading for the sandwich shop.

"That's the one," I called out. "He sent the first woman a heart-shaped box with a necklace. I think I've figured out who the bad guy is, but I'm not sure. Would you like to discuss the plot while you eat?"

Peter turned and grinned. He gave a quick nod and was soon sitting beside me, wolfing down a club sandwich and fries and discussing the finer points of the author's characterization. To me, the book was just pages filled with words that told a story. To Peter, every book was about premises and character arcs and plot points.

Before we knew it, hours had passed and we'd discussed not only my current reading material, but also the author's entire backlist and a current controversy concerning another author who wrote in the same genre.

Julie could have her tall, dark, and handsome jocks. I wanted this man whose goal in life was to create stories, too. To weave a tale that would keep a reader spellbound and guessing until the last page.

We were so different, Peter and I. Just as I'd dispelled the idea of love at first sight, I'd dismissed the idea of opposites attracting. How could you possibly spend a lifetime with someone whose interests were diametrically opposite from yours? As a psychology major, I planned to specialize in the area of testing. Cold, hard facts and raw data were my specialty. How could I be attracted to a man who dealt with wisps of ideas and characters that didn't really exist? When he spoke of his characters talking to him, I didn't know whether to nod in agreement or quickly refer him to the campus counseling clinic.

I shoved my pre-conceived notions away, ignored Julie's shallow advice, and let myself fall in love. Three months after we graduated from college, with Peter employed as a reporter for a mid-sized newspaper and me working for a private school as a testing specialist, Peter and I walked down the aisle and pledged our lives to each other.

When our first child was born two years later, Julie held him in her arms and said, "Don't say I didn't warn you." Lucas Alexander Kingsley came into the world with a shock of red hair and skin as pale as a sheet of paper.

"He's beautiful, Liz. Absolutely beautiful." She breathed in his sweet baby smell and then handed him back to me. She patted her own rounded belly. "I hope I'm half as lucky," she said as she glanced lovingly up at her gangly, six and a half foot tall husband who sported a fringe of dishwater brown hair around his baldpate.

Three years later Lucas was joined by a baby sister who proved that the laws of genetics are as fickle as the wind because she came into the world with an olive complexion and dark hair. Baby Casey completed our family and I expected life to roll merrily along with love burning bright between my husband and I.

Six years later when Peter complained of a sore throat, fatigue, and weight loss, I suggested he see our family doctor. He made an appointment, grumbling all the way that it was probably just a virus he picked up at the office. I grumbled back that it was better to be safe, just in case he had something contagious that the kids could get.

Overnight our perfect, little world turned upside down when Peter was diagnosed with lymphoma. Our usual routine gave way to a series of office visits, chemo treatments, and several hospitalizations, as a team of doctors pulled out every stop to halt the progression of the disease and rid Peter's body of it entirely.

The kids, then nine and six, were real troopers. My aunt moved in with us to look after them and help maintain some normalcy with their routines. I'd quit work after Casey was born, so my days were free for hauling Peter wherever he needed to be, or to just hold him and wipe his brow as the chemo treatments took their toll.

Thirteen months later I gripped his hand as he slipped away and the once bright light of love began its vicious scarring. Friends and family stayed by my side as I endured my husband's funeral. My aunt was a great help with the children, and Julie called me every night and let me cry over the phone to her.

"You'll get through this, Liz," she assured me. "You'll be all right."

"But I'll never fall in love again. I'll never find another Peter and even if I did, I don't ever want to hurt like this again."

"Never say never," she cautioned.

But I didn't want to hear anyone's suggestions that I'd find love again. I'd felt blessed to find love the first time and had decided that I'd used up my one chance in life.

Despite Peter's generous life insurance policy and the small amount the children and I collected from Social Security, the year after Peter died I felt the need to return to work—not only for financial reasons, but also as a distraction from my grief. The children and I had all been to counseling and were working our way through the grieving process. I felt stuck, though, and thought perhaps a change of habit might give me the shove I needed.

The school I'd worked for after graduation was delighted to have me back, but could only hire me in a part-time capacity.

"Part-time is great," I told the kids. "I can work while you are in school and be home by noon. And we'll all have the holidays and summers off together."

My first week back was a big adjustment, both in terms of work and social adjustment. Some folks openly acknowledged Peter's passing and offered their sincerest condolences. Others tiptoed around it, as if to ignore or deny he'd ever existed.

One particularly bad day, after enduring a parent's insistence that her child couldn't possibly have scored so low on a standardized reading test and that I must not know what I was doing since I was so recently widowed, I shut down my computer, grabbed my day planner and a stack of folders, and checked out early. Perhaps a manicure would calm my nerves. Or maybe a facial. I shouldered open the door leading to the parking lot and charged out, thoroughly distracted by the diversions I was contemplating.

"Ooof!" I cried as I encountered something solid and my planner, folders, and purse spilled around me. I stooped to gather my belongings and came face to face with a man I recognized as the vice principal.

"Mrs. Kingsley, I'm so sorry," he apologized as he fumbled with a tube of lipstick and a stray tampon, which had rolled a few feet away.

"No worries. I was just distracted and should have been paying more attention," I assured him, grabbing the items and stuffing them back into my purse. "And please call me Liz."

"Chris Bowles," he replied, helping me to my feet and offering a firm handshake. "I understand you've just returned to The Providence

School after being at home for a few years, and if there's any way I can help, please let me know." He stepped back and cleared the way for me to proceed. "Feel free to call me at home, too. Any time. And if you want to chat during the day, my office door is always open. Maybe I'll see you around in the cafeteria."

Was he flirting with me? I'd been out of the dating pool for so long I wasn't sure if I'd even recognize a come-on. And besides, I was a woman with two young children, who had been widowed for. . . .

Had it been a year and a half? The wound still seemed as new and fresh as that day in the hospital when Peter closed his eyes and never woke up again.

I was an attractive woman and surely Chris Bowles knew my marital status. He was held in high regard by his peers and didn't seem the type to hit on a married woman. My initial shock abated as I slid behind the wheel of my car and twisted the key in the ignition. Maybe I wouldn't call him at home or even seek him out at school, but if the handsome vice principal wanted to join me for coffee in the teachers' lounge, maybe I could paste a smile on my face and test the waters again.

Coffee in the teachers' lounge led to lunch at a local café and that led to dinner at a cozy bistro known for its romantic ambience. I was always open with my situation and talked frequently about my children. Any man I dated had to understand that I was part of a package deal. While Chris had never made any sort of romantic overtures, I wanted to be sure he understood exactly what I expected from a relationship.

I also learned that he was widowed as well, but he'd been alone three times as long as I had. His wife had been killed when a drunk driver broadsided their car. Her side of the car caught the full impact of the crash and she was killed immediately.

"If only I'd taken a different route home," he said as he told the story. "If I'd driven a little slower we'd have been at that crossroad later. I beat myself up with what ifs for way too long." He sipped slowly at the cup of coffee he'd ordered with dessert.

"I know what you mean. I still wonder if I should have picked up on Peter's illness earlier. Maybe if I'd paid closer attention I'd have seen he was losing weight."

"Hindsight is twenty-twenty, but that doesn't change the facts. And the fact now is that I'm resolved to live life to the fullest and maybe even marry again one day."

I nodded silently, still not sure I could ever take that step again. As much as I enjoyed Chris's company, I didn't know if I could ever let myself become as involved emotionally—and physically—as I had with Peter.

We continued to see each other outside of work and the shell I'd built around me began to crumble, especially after Chris took such an interest in Lucas and Casey. He spent hours with Lucas helping him construct part of his science project, and when Casey's dance recital fell on the night we had scheduled for dinner, he tagged along and applauded more loudly than any parent.

As Easter approached, I felt myself sliding into the usual funk that surrounded the anniversary of Peter's death. It didn't seem to matter that Easter's date varied from year to year. I always associated it with great loss instead of celebrating it for what it was—a symbol of hope.

"Chris's coming over on Sunday to help us hide Easter eggs," Casey told me the week beforehand. "He said he was the best egg hider in his neighborhood growing up and said there was always at least one egg nobody found until a couple of weeks later."

"Yeah," Lucas piped in. "I can't wait! It's gonna be awesome to have him here."

Since when did my pre-teen son have an interest in hiding Easter eggs? He'd strayed from the tradition after Peter died, despite me urging him to help his sister hunt for hers. Perhaps he was finally realizing he should help keep traditions alive for Casey and he'd had a change of heart.

I'd invited Chris over for Easter breakfast and when he showed up at my front door, he held out a white straw basket decorated with silk flowers and ribbons. An empty basket.

"What's this for?" I asked as I took the basket from him.

"It's for hunting eggs, silly," Lucas chimed in from behind me. "Chris asked me if you had a basket and I told him no."

"But I don't need to hunt for eggs," I protested. "That's just for you and Casey."

"Everybody needs to hunt for eggs, Mommy." Casey squeezed between the door and me and smiled at Chris. "You don't want to be a bad sport, do you?"

"No," I drawled. "But breakfast is almost ready and we need to eat first. Then you'll hunt for eggs."

All three of them glared at me. "We'll hunt for eggs," I corrected.

The children wolfed their pancakes and eggs as if they hadn't had a meal in days. Even Chris ate more quickly than usual and were I a suspicious woman, I'd have been . . . well, suspicious.

After clearing the table and loading the dishwasher, Casey shoved the decorated basket into my hands and grabbed her own. "Time to hunt for eggs now!" she said and skipped across the house and out the front door.

As I stood on my front porch I could see bright spots of color dotting the lawn and mulched beds.

"Go ahead, Mommy! You take the flower beds and look there," Casey said as she plucked a plastic egg from under an azalea bush.

I played along and my basket was soon filled with eggs. Lucas and I fought over who found the blue one under the maple tree first, and Casey squealed when she discovered the red one she'd found in the mailbox contained candy.

"Have we found them all yet, Chris?" Lucas asked excitedly.

All our baskets were filled to the brim with eggs. Surely no more were hidden in our yard. Chris let his gaze wander from one side of the property to the other, letting it settle briefly on my favorite magnolia tree.

"Nope, there's one more left. And it's a special egg, too," he explained.

"You kids go find it then." I sat on the front steps and waited for them to start scrambling to find the last egg.

"No, you get this one, Mom," Lucas said. "Casey and I already have special eggs. See?" He held up an oversized one that had been filled with movie passes and Casey displayed another that housed a gift card to her favorite clothing store.

"Yeah, Liz. This one is yours." Chris pulled me from my sitting position and winked. Just what did he have up his sleeve?

Remembering that he'd paused when he looked at the magnolia tree, I made my way to the tall tree with limbs that draped nearly to the ground. I circled once, twice, and then I spotted it—a sequin-encrusted egg nestled in the branches. Carefully I reached in and lifted the egg. As I pulled it toward me, something rattled inside and I tugged gently to open it and discover what surprise the egg held.

"Here, let me," Chris said when the egg refused to yield. With a twist he had it open—to reveal a sparkling diamond ring.

I gasped in surprise and looked at my children, who stood behind Chris with grins on their faces.

"You knew about this, didn't you?" I squinted and sent them a mock-angry look.

"Yep. We did good, didn't we, Chris?" Lucas rocked back on his heels and smiled brightly.

"You guys did great," he said as he bumped knuckles with Lucas. "You were egg-ceptional, as a matter of fact."

Then he turned back to me and knelt on the grass. Tears gathered behind my lids and I blinked furiously to hold them at bay.

"Liz, I know how important your kids are to you and I thought maybe I should get their blessing before I made the next move." He looked over his shoulder at Lucas and Casey and they nodded. "Now that I have their okay, I want to ask you if you'll do me the honor of being my wife."

"I egg-cept," I answered softly, and then giggled. Chris stood and pulled me into his arms. I lost the battle with my tears and they flowed freely, as my children hurried to my side and joined in the group hug.

Grandma was right. True love burns the brightest and leaves a deep scar. But true love can happen more than once and I was lucky enough to find it on the day that celebrates hope and eternal life.

THE END

HOME SWEET HOME
I'm Where I Belong

Peeling paint flaked onto my black slacks, I sat on the aging swing awaiting Aunt Ruby's attorney to arrive with the keys that would open the house she'd left me in her will. Despite the state of disrepair, her flowers still bloomed among weeds in front of the house. I remembered an Easter Sunday when I helped her gather the best ones to take to her beloved church where they would grace the table in front of the pulpit.

Regarding the house, my first instinct had been to stay where I was and call a local realtor to sell the place. Then, after talking to Winston Bennett, the attorney, I learned the house had come with stipulations.

s   "It needs work, Mrs. Randall," he said. "Your aunt specified that it was to be restored before it was put on the market and she left some money for that purpose."

"What if I don't want to restore it? What if I don't have the time?"

"The house will go to her church," he said.

"That's totally unfair. I don't even live in the same state, and I can't just walk out on my job. Do you know how hard it is to find a job these days?"

"I'm sorry, but there is nothing I can do about it. As executor of her will it is my job to make sure her wishes are carried out exactly."

"I'll call you back," I told him.

I considered my situation. The studio apartment I lived in was rented on a month-to-month basis. It wasn't as though I had a hot career going; I worked in a restaurant and could wait tables anywhere. There was no family to speak of. I made a decision. If my ten-year-old Ford was up to the trip I'd go.

The next day I called the attorney and told him when to expect me. Afterward I gave notice to my landlady and my employer, packed my few belongings, filled the car with gas, and got a map that would show me the fastest way to Dobson Mills, Georgia.

I was born in Dobson Mills, and for the first seven years of my life I lived two doors down from Aunt Ruby and Uncle Bill Stevens. Sometimes I thought that those were the happiest days of my life. Nothing since had measured up. At Momma's insistence our family had moved up North because she thought Daddy could get a better job and make more money.

Things hadn't worked out so well. When I was ten Daddy left us. He and Momma got divorced. She remarried a couple of years later and started a new family with John Williams, my stepfather. Momma was never really close to me before she remarried, but after, she barely acknowledged my existence.

When anyone in Daddy's family wrote and asked me to visit during holidays or the summer she tore up the letters. "You're not going to see that man's family and listen to them tell lies about me!" she'd scream.

I grew up feeling apart and lonely. At age twenty, I fell in love with a man who was a customer at the diner where I worked and we later married. Though I loved Thomas with all my heart, I hadn't been his first choice. When we married he was rebounding from a long-term relationship with a girl he'd loved most of his life.

Thomas Randall and I had been married eight months when we went to visit his family for the holidays. At a New Year's Eve party he ran into his old girlfriend. Midway thorough the party I couldn't find Thomas. When the party ended one of the guests drove me back to the Randall house.

Two days later, Thomas returned and asked me for a divorce. He said he could never be happy without Dee, his old love. We didn't have much, but he told me I was welcome to all of it if he could just have his freedom. I gave him the divorce.

Four years passed since that time. I moved from menial job to menial job without any real purpose in my life. Momma and John moved west for his health. Soon after Momma moved away I heard through a letter from Aunt Ruby that Daddy had died of lung cancer.

I attended Daddy's funeral and spent hours talking to Aunt Ruby. She was just as I remembered her; jovial, smiling, and kindhearted, despite the tragedies of her own life and the terrible losses.

When the letter came telling me Aunt Ruby had passed, I didn't have enough money to go to her funeral. I managed to scrape up enough to send some flowers, trying to make them as much like the ones in her garden as possible. Then, a few weeks later, I got a letter from a lawyer telling me that Aunt Ruby had left me her house. I'd imagined it would look like it had the last time I saw it. Unfortunately, I was wrong.

Glancing at my Timex watch I saw that the lawyer was almost an hour late and wondered if he planned to come at all. If he didn't come I wondered what I would do. I'd spent most of my money on gas for the trip. I couldn't afford a motel room. As the sun began to set I became more and more anxious.

A few cars drove down the street, pulling into driveways, or parking at the curb, which was lined with mimosa and pecan trees. Some of the old houses were gone. In their places stood smaller, newer cottages, or overgrown vacant lots. A brick duplex had replaced the house I'd lived in.

Just as I made up my mind to break a window and climb through it so I'd have a place to stay for the night, a car pulled up and parked in front of the house. A well-dressed man stepped out of the car and took long strides up the walkway.

"Mrs. Randall, I am so sorry I'm late. I got held up in court. I'm Winston Bennett." He held out his hand to shake mine.

"Good thing you came," I said. "I was about to bust out a window and climb inside. I don't have enough money for a motel room."

He laughed. Obviously this well dressed attorney had never known what it was like to have nothing and no place to go. I stood and brushed the paint chips from my pants and walked with him to the front door.

"Your aunt's house is fully furnished," he said. "Of course, the furniture is quite old, and I'm sure you'll want to bring in your own things."

"I don't have any things, Mr. Bennett. All I own is my car, a couple of boxes of letters and stuff, and two suitcases of clothes."

He unlocked the door and opened it for me. The old hallway was dark. He flicked on a light switch and I felt as though I'd been transported back in time. Sitting in the hallway was a desk like they used to have in schoolrooms. Under it was a telephone directory, and on the desk sat a phone.

"It's exactly the way I remember it," I said.

"Miss Ruby never changed much," he said. "Not that she didn't want to though. I have a box of all the clippings she cut out of magazines, which she intended to use as ideas to fix this place up."

"Doesn't look like she got around to decorating," I said.

"After Mr. Bill passed her health started to fail. All the same, she'd have me bring her magazines so she could look at them and clip the pictures she liked."

"You sound as though you knew my aunt and uncle well," I said.

"I knew them all my life," he said. "Did you notice the big house across the street?"

Of course I'd noticed it. Unless I'd been blind I couldn't have missed it. "Yes," I said. "Did you grow up there?" I remembered that the richest family in the neighborhood had owned it at one time.

"I grew up in the servant's quarters in back of it," he said. "My mother worked for the owners in lieu of rent." An obvious question would have been to ask how he happened to end up as an attorney driving a new BMW, and wearing an expensive suit. "You probably don't remember me, but we used to play together. You and Louise would badger me into having tea parties with you in Miss Ruby's back yard."

I remembered my cousin Louise. She was a year older than I was and had died at age twelve to Leukemia. I learned of her death from my grandmother on my father's side. Louise had an older brother, Billy, Jr. I remembered him vaguely. He played sports and didn't have time for little girls' foolishness.

Billy had died young as well, though his death was due to drowning. I didn't know the details; only that he had died the summer after he graduated from high school.

"I was so young when we lived here that I don't remember too many people," I said.

"Winnie, Winnie, short and skinny," he said. "I still have nightmares about being called those names." There was a soft smile playing on his lips.

I did remember. "No! I can't believe it. You're Winnie?"

"Yes, I am, Ruth Anne. Hope you don't mind if I call you Ruth Anne."

"It's a lot better than what Louise and I used to call you. Dear heavens, you sure have changed. Nobody would call you short and skinny now."

"I've grown a few inches and put on a couple of pounds," he said, still smiling.

He'd grown more than a few inches, and every pound he'd put on had gone to all the right places. "I wish you'd told me who you were when you wrote me."

"I was afraid you'd forgotten. Besides, we lawyers like doing things all legal and formal."

"Since you're doing this transaction all legal and formal; mind telling me why Aunt Ruby won't let me sell the house outright? I could use the money. Winnie, I'm flat broke."

"Ruby wanted you to spend some time here. She said you've had a hard life and thought you could use the rest. You know how she always had her cookie jar funds; well, she had one set up to pay to fix the house so it would bring more money if you decided to sell it."

"How am I supposed to live in the meantime? I don't have a job."

"Can you use a computer?"

"Not really. I took a course in high school but I've forgotten most of what they taught me. For the past few years I've waited tables."

"Ruth Anne, I'm sure we can find a job for you. As for fixing the place up, I promised Miss Ruby I'd give you a hand. Structurally the place is in good shape. Your Uncle Bill was handy and could fix about anything. All you need is some paint on the walls, an upgrade in the kitchen, and a little landscaping."

"That doesn't sound like too much to do," I said, thinking that maybe a month and I could sell the house, make a nice profit, and go about my life.

"Let me show you the rest of the place," Winnie said. I followed him from room to room, mentally calculating how much money and work would be needed to upgrade the house.

"She sure loved wallpaper," I said, dreading the misery of removing it.

"Some of it is the same as when Louise and Billy, Jr. were alive," he said. "Miss Ruby could never bring herself to change their rooms."

"Poor Aunt Ruby," I said. "She had such sadness in her life."

"Never in this house, though."

His remark puzzled me. Aunt Ruby had lost both of her children and the only man she'd ever loved. There had been so many times she and Uncle Bill struggled just to put food on the table. I remembered Granny once saying that she didn't know how Aunt Ruby and Uncle Bill were going to keep their home after he was laid off at his job.

"Winnie, I think the struggles she went through qualify for being very sad."

"Let's go take a seat in the living room," he said. "I want to tell you some things about Miss Ruby that you might not know."

He turned on the lights and took a seat on the fat, faded recliner while I settled upon the sofa with its many colorful pillows.

"When I was a boy my life was hard," he said. "Daddy drank and often beat Momma and me. Sometimes Momma would come here to Miss Ruby's to hide out when Daddy was in a bad mood. Miss Ruby had a rule. If anybody was sad they had to be sad on the front porch or the back porch. Inside the house was for being happy."

What an odd philosophy, I thought. When I was growing up all I knew was screaming and crying in our house. Momma and Daddy argued all the time. Later, after they divorced, Momma cried or yelled at me. After she married John things weren't much better. How could a family limit their misery to outside of the house?

"You look puzzled, Ruth Anne."

"You'll have to pardon me, but it does seem odd."

"That's the way Miss Ruby wanted things. She said the happiest day of her life, besides the day she married, and the days her children were born, was the day she and Mr. Bill moved into this house. They laughed and danced from room to room, happy to have a home of their own."

"She said she told Mr. Bill that the house was always going to be just that way. It was a happy place. If trouble came, it would have to stay outside. I remember when Louise died and I saw Miss Ruby sitting on the swing, crying her eyes out. It was raining something dreadful and my momma asked her if she didn't want to go inside. She shook her head and said she wasn't going to bring sorrow into her house."

His story made me wonder once more why she'd left the house to me. My entire life had been one big load of sorrow, and I didn't see it looking up any time soon. If Aunt Ruby hadn't wanted sorrow in her house she should have left it to someone happier than I was. Could this be her way of forcing me to be happy? From the way things were I could see a lot of my future being spent on the front porch in the swing, honoring Aunt Ruby's rule about sorrow staying outside.

"This is such an old area," I said. "Even if I fix the house up, do you think I'll make anything off the sale of it?"

"You'd be surprised. This area is starting to become chic again. Especially the older houses like this one."

I remembered something my grandmother had told me about the neighborhood. Once Georgia Avenue and the surrounding streets were considered upscale; there was a recreational park less than a mile away and the streetcar line was a three-block walk. People flocked to the area and most of them were wealthy so they built fine, big houses.

As the mills grew and choked out smoke and pollution, the wealthy residents moved away to the suburbs. Houses fell into affordable disrepair; many became boarding houses when the Depression hit. My grandfather bought the house that once stood next door. Aunt Ruby said she'd grown up sitting on her parents' porch, wishing that she owned the house that she and Uncle Bill eventually bought.

It was a mess when they bought it. Fortunately Uncle Bill was skillful and was able to repair everything that needed fixing while Aunt Ruby decorated and planted the most beautiful garden on the street.

"You must be starving," Winnie said, bringing me back to the present day.

"Did you guess, or did my growling stomach give me away?"

"How about I take you to dinner?"

"I'd love it. I'm sure there's nothing here to eat."

"There's food," he said. "Lots and lots of canned goods. And a freezer full of pecans."

"Are those things safe to eat?"

"You bet. Miss Ruby was always careful when she canned, and the pecans came from her own trees. There are four out back and the two beside the curb. Until she got sick she'd collect them and shell them to make holiday candy."

"I'd still rather go to a restaurant," I said.

Though my clothes were wrinkled they were not much worse than anything else I owned, but I wasn't going to dinner without washing up first and fixing my hair and makeup. Winnie waited patiently as I got ready.

We drove to town. I remembered some of the large department

stores, which now stood empty. Granny used to take me shopping there once in a while and I loved the scent of the perfume counter.

The restaurant Winnie took me to was nice, and I felt immediately underdressed. Frankly, I wasn't used to being waited upon. I was usually the one taking the orders. Winnie suggested a few of his favorites. All sounded good, so I let him order for us. He selected a bottle of wine, which I am certain cost more than my blouse.

"You look a lot like Miss Ruby when she was your age," he said.

"How would you know? You're just a few years older than I am."

"Scrapbooks. It was one of her hobbies, and when I visited her we would spend hours cutting and pasting pictures into those scrapbooks. They're at the house. You should take a look at them sometime. Your father's family history is all there for you to see."

"My father ran out on us when I was a little girl," I said, hearing the bitterness of my words.

"There are always two sides to every story. If I hadn't known that before becoming an attorney, I sure as heck know it now."

"He never came to see me after he left," I said.

"Ruth Anne, there might have been reasons he didn't contact you. I know for a fact that Miss Ruby sent you a birthday card every year on your birthday, and every year the card came back unopened. She was really hurt that you didn't invite her to your wedding. Especially after she helped pay for it."

"Aunt Ruby didn't pay for my wedding. Momma paid for it and never let me forget it. Her one condition was that none of Daddy's family would be invited."

"I have the cancelled check, Ruth Anne."

I drank some of my wine, feeling worse by the minute. It would have been just like Momma to lie to me about the wedding. She had always hated and resented Aunt Ruby. Actually, Momma hated and resented anyone and everyone that Daddy or I ever loved. She treated John, my stepfather, Lacey, my half-sister, and Trevor, my half-brother the same way. If they liked someone, Momma hated that person and would criticize the poor soul for hours. She was possessive to a fault, but I never thought she'd go so far as to lie about money sent to me from my father's family.

"Aunt Ruby actually helped pay for my wedding?"

"She sent a check for five thousand dollars," he said. "She'd kept the money in one of her green jars, saving it for Louise's wedding. After Louise died Ruby kept the money for you."

"Where did she get the money? Surely Uncle Bill didn't make that much fixing busses."

He smiled. "Did you ever eat one of her cakes?"

I seemed to remember a birthday cake with five candles, decorated

78

in the shape of a playhouse with pink icing and green cotton candy for the lawn. "Louise's fifth birthday cake," I said. "I'll never forget it."

"Your aunt made cakes for years—pies, too, and sinful candy. My favorite thing she made was her gingerbread man cookie."

"I remember the gingerbread men. She used to let Louise and I put jellybeans on them. Aunt Ruby said they were prettier than raisins. We'd cut small jelly beans in half and make eyes and buttons."

"That was the way she earned the money she kept in her various jars."

We laughed. Winnie proposed a toast to Aunt Ruby. We clicked our glasses together and drank in her honor. At that moment something sleeping deep in my soul awoke. I could feel laughter and joy. They were feelings I hadn't fully known since I was a little girl, playing at Aunt Ruby's house, which was now my house.

"I had so much fun there," I said. "She and Uncle Bill never argued. I can remember when he'd come home from work and plant a big kiss on her. Then he'd ask her what smelled so good and she'd tell him what she cooked for dinner. He always made a fuss over everything she made."

"I remember that, too," Winnie said. "Lots of nights I ate supper there. Mr. Bill was my little league coach and he'd take me home with him after practice or a game. I think he did it so he could be sure I would have something to eat. Daddy drank up every cent he could get his hands on."

Our meal was served and I enjoyed it thoroughly. We chatted as we ate, and talked about the renovations ahead. I was still worried about decades of wallpaper. Winnie assured me that it wouldn't be a problem.

After dinner he drove me to the grocery store and insisted upon paying for my purchases. Next we went to the house. He helped me put the groceries away and told me about each idiosyncrasy of the old house.

"I have court early tomorrow, but as soon as I can I'll come here and take you to the hardware store to get some stuff to remove the wallpaper. I'll help you get it off. Miss Ruby would haunt me if I let anything happen to you."

"Thank you, Winnie," I said.

"Ruth Anne, just one little favor I have to ask you; I'm thirty and a respected attorney. People don't call me Winnie anymore. It's Winn."

I laughed. "Winnie, Winnie, short and skinny."

"Don't make me have to pull your pigtail," he said, grinning.

"I don't have pigtails anymore."

He winked and turned to go. As I watched him leave I found that I was laughing—I was happy. So much time had passed since I'd felt happy. Maybe there was magic in Aunt Ruby's old house.

The next day I spent hours in each room trying to decide how to redecorate it. I'd forgotten how cheerful Louise's room had been. It was hard to imagine a child suffering the agony of her illness in such a pretty room. Pink had always been her favorite color. The walls were decorated with tiny pink roses, and a handmade bedspread with matching flowers covered the bed.

On shelves were dolls dressed in silk and feathers, and stored in the closet was a dollhouse that looked exactly like the cake I remembered. Louise had lived such a short time, yet those years had been filled with love that I could only imagine. She'd had things I could only dream of. Most of all, she had loving parents.

I felt sad and immediately walked out the back door to shed my tears. Aunt Ruby's house was a house of laughter and joy. I wasn't going to break the tradition.

Winnie. . .pardon me, Winn came over around five and I shared some of my ideas with him. He liked most of them.

"Want to see what your aunt thought should be done?" he asked.

"I suppose you'll show me anyway."

He went to her bedroom, which was now my bedroom, and got a pretty pink hatbox and brought it to the dining room table. Inside were clipped pictures from home improvement magazines. He spread them out.

"She wanted to completely re-do the kitchen," he said, showing me a glossy photograph of a gorgeous kitchen with a large cooking island. "She thought it would be a good idea to knock out the side wall that leads to the laundry room, and move the laundry room closer to the bathroom where the dirty clothes hamper is."

"Makes sense," I said.

"She said she could just imagine herself making dozens and dozens of cakes on that big kitchen island."

"I wonder if she could imagine me making cakes on it. I'm not the cook she was."

"Ruth Anne, she wanted you to be happy. Whatever you decide to do with this house is fine, as long as you do something."

"Winn, where are the scrapbooks you told me about?"

"Under the bed in plastic boxes," he said. "I'll get them for you before I leave."

We had bought a bottle of wine the night before. We opened it and drank as we snacked on cheese and crackers. Winn told me about his current court case, and I sat transfixed, imagining him cross-examine a witness.

"This is not a proper question," I said, "but how did you manage to pay for law school?"

He gave me the smile, which I'd decided was about the cutest smile in the entire world. "That would be another of Miss Ruby's special jars. She saved for college for Louise and Billy, Jr. since they were born. After Louise died she kept saving for Billy to go to college. He wanted to wait a year so he could buy a car before going. I think he hoped she'd give him the money for that, but she put her foot down."

"On the Fourth of July before he was to go to college we were all at a picnic at Dawkins Lake when Billy decided to impress a girl who was visiting for the summer. There was an old rope hanging from a high tree limb over the lake. Everyone told Billy it was too dangerous, but he wouldn't listen and climbed the rope. Billy made it to the limb, but the limb was rotten and broke. He fell into the shallow water, hit is head on a rock, and died instantly."

"I always thought he'd drowned," I said.

"Miss Ruby spent a lot of the summer on the porch swing after Billy died. A few years later, after I graduated from high school, I applied for grants and got a couple. I told her about my plans to go to college. One day I was cutting grass next door to earn some money and she called me over."

"The college jar," I said.

He nodded. "She knew if Daddy found out I had any cash he'd take it and get drunk. Miss Ruby had me drive her to the bank, where we opened a checking account in my name, using her address. My father never knew how I paid for college. Once I left here I wrote to Miss Ruby every week, and she always wrote back. I still have all of her letters, and she kept mine."

"She was an amazing woman."

"More than you know. She kept that college jar going until I graduated from law school. My mother died when I was in college. On my graduation day it was Miss Ruby and Mr. Bill sitting there watching me get my diploma. They were always my second family. Actually, they were the family I wished I had."

"I got Louise's wedding fund and you got Billy's college fund," I said. "I'm glad that at least one of us was around to show her some appreciation, and that her hard earned money paid off for one of us."

"If you want to show her your appreciation, make her house the way she dreamed it would be. Put your love and your heart into it the way she did. Even if you sell it, at least make it pretty before you put it on the market."

I nodded. "It's the least I can do."

We finished the wine and I made a quick dinner; not much, just sandwiches and some canned soup. Winn and I drove to the hardware store and got wallpaper remover and some color swatches.

I was going to work my hardest to make Aunt Ruby's home

beautiful. However, I had to eat and pay the utility bills, so that meant getting a job.

Winn helped me find a job at a dress shop owned by the aunt of his secretary. The shop was open four days a week, which left three days to work on the house. Weekends Winn came and helped. Together we cleared the closets and donated many useful things to charity. Some things I put in the attic because they were too precious to part with. One was the pink dollhouse.

We stripped walls of fading paper, and then painted them. Weeks became months and I looked forward to waking each morning to a new and happy day. My job was fun and Jeanne, the owner, treated me like family. I met Aunt Ruby's neighbors and each one had a story of some way she helped them. Uncle Bill's poker buddies volunteered to lend a hand with the renovations, and a few gave me good ideas.

More than anything, though, there was Winn. We laughed and teased each other, much as we had when we were children. Sometimes we went out to dinner, or to a movie. Other times he sat with me while I looked at the scrapbooks.

"These pictures are so old," I said looking at one of the books.

"They're your ancestors, Ruth Anne. There is some part of each one of them in you."

Other books showed relatives in uniforms, dressed to go to war and defend the Country. I saw pictures of family gatherings and picnics with a cemetery in the background.

"What a peculiar place to have a picnic," I said.

"That's when they used to clean the graves, pull the weeds, and honor their dead. Miss Ruby said they went every year when she was a girl, and she could tell you who was buried in each grave, and a little something about them."

I was impressed. My aunt had known bits and pieces about all of her ancestors, yet I didn't even know where my own mother had been born. We simply didn't talk about those things. The past was just that—the past. Like so many of my generation, my head was on trivial entertainment.

"I'm going to start a scrapbook," I told Winn. "It'll be all about this house. I'm going to find old pictures of it, and as we renovate it, I'm going to take pictures of it. And I want to landscape the house exactly the way Aunt Ruth had it."

He moaned and shook his head before laughing. "Woman, you are a lot more like your aunt than you'll ever know. I'll order some bulbs so you'll have gorgeous flowers by Easter."

Though there were dozens of things to do, the next day I started weeding the garden and preparing it for planting season. Winn spent all of his free time with me. I asked him why he bothered when he should be going out on dates, or having a good time with friends. He would look at me and smile—that was my answer.

Through the seasons I pampered and decorated the house. Winn and I scoured antique shops, and took long drives to find just the right touches. My scrapbook grew thicker, and so did my interest in Winn. The day we painted the front porch swing was the day I realized I'd fallen in love. It was a strange day that began with a call from my mother.

"Ruth Anne, your sister is getting married and it would be nice if you could help pay for some of the wedding expenses," Momma said. "I know you inherited that old house of your aunt's."

"Momma, I'm living in the house. I haven't made a dime off it. I have a little money put back from my job. I could send some of that."

"How much?"

"Would a thousand dollars help?"

"I paid a lot more than that for your wedding," she said.

"Momma, it was Aunt Ruby who sent the money to pay for my wedding, and I know you didn't spend the entire five thousand dollars she sent. My dress was secondhand, the church only charged us for cleaning, and you bummed flowers from Ann Thompson down the street."

"You are such a liar. I paid for that wedding with money that should have been used for better things considering how short your marriage lasted."

"You're the liar. I know about the wedding money. I've seen the cancelled check. You didn't spend a dime out of your pocket for my wedding. I'll help my sister because she is my sister, but I'll send the money directly to her."

"You were never a grateful child. If it hadn't been for you I could have married someone a lot better than your daddy. That whole family thought they were better than I was, but they weren't."

"Momma, I don't know why you married Daddy. You never seemed to love him. You never seemed to love anybody."

"I married him because of you. My daddy made me marry him because he got me pregnant. If I had the money I'd have gotten an abortion, but my daddy didn't believe in abortions."

That was the most I ever heard from her about her life with my father. No one had ever told me that my mother and father had to get married. Hearing her cruel words stung me deeply; taking away the good feelings that had grown over the past months.

As I felt the sting of tears I slammed down the phone and ran outside to the porch. No tears were shed in Aunt Ruby's house, so I sat on the swing and wept. I was still sobbing when Winn arrived.

"Ruthie, what's wrong?"

I shook my head. Shame filled me. Though the sin was not mine, I still felt the shame of being conceived out of wedlock. Winn reached for my hands and pulled me to my feet. He gathered me into his arms and held me while I cried until there were no more tears. Using his fresh handkerchief, he wiped my face, and then kissed my cheek as gently as one would kiss a wounded child. I felt the flip-flop of my heart, telling me I was in love.

"I think you'll feel a lot better after we paint the swing," he said.

"I'm sure I will," I said, gazing into his eyes. Together we painted the swing. I wanted to say more, but fear of rejection held me back. All of my life I'd known rejection. One more would destroy me. It was better to be Winn's friend than to have him tell me he could never love me.

I kept my secret as I continued to work on the house. One morning in early spring, Winn came over. In his hand was a daffodil. When I opened the door he handed it to me.

"Where did you get it?" I asked.

"From your garden. Come look. Some have bloomed early."

I raced outside, wearing my nightgown and robe, completely barefoot, and feeling the nip of the air and the damp chill of the grass on my feet as I stood in amazement that the bulbs I'd planted had bloomed. "I thought it would be next year at the earliest before they came up," I said.

"You have a green thumb, and this is excellent soil."

Easter was only a few weeks away. If the rest of the flowers were as lovely as these, I knew what I would do. I hadn't yet visited Aunt Ruby's church, but it was time, and I wouldn't go empty handed. Once more, flowers from her garden would grace the table in front of the pulpit.

"Winn, will you take me to church on Easter?" I asked.

"I would have taken you before if you said you wanted to go." He bent down and sniffed the sweet flowers. "This is amazing, Ruthie. You've turned the house and the garden into a show place, and you've done it all under budget."

"I had a budget?" It was news to me.

"Renovations jar," he said. "You have close to six grand left over."

"You never told me."

"Miss Ruby made me promise not to. She said she wanted you to do the house exactly the way you wanted it. If you needed more money, then I was to give it to you."

"Why you?"

"Repayment jar," he said. "I wanted to pay her back for the college money. She told me to put the money in a jar and keep it so that someday I could do something good for a deserving person who might need it."

"I guess I better start one of those jars, too," I said. We walked back into the house. I put on a pot of coffee. Winn sat at the kitchen island, watching me for the longest time.

He gazed down and there was a somewhat sad look on his face. "I know a great realtor. I'll give you her name."

"Why would I want a realtor?"

"To list the house. It's finished now and you can sell it. I know the market is slow, but this place will bring top dollar."

"Winn, why would I want to sell my home? This house holds every happy moment I've ever known in my entire life. The best things that have ever happened to me happened within these walls."

When he looked up I was stunned to see tears in his eyes. "Guess I'd better go outside," he said.

"Are you sad? Are you sorry I'm staying?"

"Not at all, but this is a tear free zone, so say something funny quick," he said.

"Okay. How's this? I'm in love with you." I'd waited long enough to let him know how I felt. If he rejected me, then I'd deal with it.

"Ruth, that had better not be your idea of a joke!"

"Why not?"

"Because I'm in love with you, too, and the way I feel certainly isn't a joke. I think I fell in love with you when you first came here, but I didn't want to influence your decision in case you didn't want to stay."

I wanted to stay, and I wanted to love him forever. On Easter we took the bouquet from Ruby's garden to the church. I met her minister and apologized for not attending services sooner. He was kind, and when Winn and I told him we wanted to get married there, he made sure that all of Ruby's friends knew about it.

Winn and I were married, and we share the house that came to mean so much to the both of us. Aunt Ruby's rule is still in place. Above our door there is a sign that reads, "Happy House," and forever that is what it will be, because it brought me home to the man that I will always love.

THE END

EASTER LOVE
I Hopped Into His Heart

Working as the assistant to the marketing manager for a busy suburban shopping mall came with its own set of challenges—and perks. On any given day, my boss, Janice, might have me serving coffee and cookies to local senior citizens, or running a soundboard for a hip fashion show.

Distributing educational materials to teenagers, or overseeing a playgroup for toddlers. Collaborating with local artisans, setting up displays of their work, or organizing seasonal craft sales. Calling bingo, or running a shuffleboard tournament for a large crowd. Or marking Halloween, Christmas, and countless other holidays with appropriately costumed characters and giveaways.

One thing was for sure—the work was never boring. There was always something happening to keep me hopping.

Sometimes literally. On the Tuesday before Easter, the actor I'd hired to play the Easter Bunny all week in the mall called to tell me he'd broken his leg and wouldn't be able to honor his contract.

All of my efforts to line up a last-minute substitute failed, so I was forced to don the bunny suit myself, much to Janice's amusement.

"You look very dapper, Paulette," she commented, straightening my ears.

"I look ridiculous," I muttered, picking up the beribboned basketful of foil-wrapped chocolate eggs on my desk. "And I need sweatbands already!"

Janice hid a snicker with a nicely manicured hand. "I'll pick some up for you at the sporting goods store," she promised. "Anything else you'll need?"

"Other than a new job? How about a rear-view mirror?"

"You'll be fine," she said airily. "How hard could walking around the mall be?"

Peering at her through the openings in the mask, I wondered if she was right.

It wasn't long until I found out. Navigating in the outfit was a nightmare. The huge paws covering my sensible sneakers were clumsy in the extreme, and I had no peripheral vision at all. Surrounded by children with outstretched palms, I was completely at their mercy. And the little devils knew it, judging by the number of tweaks my poor, fluffy tail received! Sweatbands helped; I could at least take advantage of the limited vision and comfort I did have without perspiration running in my eyes and soaking my forearms.

Soon, I was happily wandering around the mall, visiting merchants, and spreading good cheer, dancing when I felt like it, to the amusement of almost everyone.

I was feeling much better about the whole thing until I was blindsided near the food court.

The offender was a small child—that was all I could tell. He or she hit my midsection at a dead run, flung their arms around me, and hugged me so hard that I completely lost my breath.

At least I didn't fall, I thought dizzily. Or drop the basket!

"Max Dobson, you come back here right now!"

A deep male voice, sounding both exasperated and embarrassed, reached me through the haze. A strong hand gripped my arm, steadying me.

"Are you okay?"

"Yes, thanks," I mumbled.

"Daddy, it's a girl bunny!" Max said gleefully, resting his head on my bosom.

"Daddy" cleared his throat; evidently to hide his understandably amused response to that announcement.

"Let go of her, young man," he said, sounding stern. But I knew that if I could see his face, he'd be smiling.

When Max didn't obey right away, I resorted to desperate measures. "Would you like a chocolate egg?" I asked, hoping to facilitate my release.

"Is it okay if I have one, Daddy?"

"Yes. But only one."

Max turned me loose with obvious reluctance, and I handed over a purple-and-yellow spotted egg with great fanfare, bowing after he'd accepted it. "Thank you, Miss Bunny," he said, beginning to unwrap it.

"You're welcome." I peered through the mask at him. He was probably five years old, with straight, shiny blond hair and startlingly blue eyes.

"Sorry about the body check," his father said. "He does have some manners, but he doesn't know his own strength."

I gave my attention to the owner of that extremely attractive voice. It was tinged with an intriguing hint of a southern accent, and I wanted to see if the rest of him lived up to its promise.

"No problem," I said, wishing I could see him better. I had only a brief impression of dark brown hair and eyes and an appealingly boyish smile, and then the two of them were heading off into the mall, hand-in-hand.

It figured that the first time I ran across a friendly male in the mall's vicinity, he'd be married—and I'd be incognito in a furry suit.

Just my luck.

Over the next few days, I ran into Max and his father several times in the mall. Along the way, I learned that "Daddy"'s name was Ryan. The source was completely unexpected. Tracy, one of my regular bingo ladies, apparently lived in the same apartment building as the Dobsons. She didn't know anything else about Ryan, but claimed she'd never seen Max's mother at any time in the entire year she'd lived there.

Which meant I was free to check Ryan out, guilt-free.

Being in costume at every encounter made that possible, and I liked what I saw. Despite his habit of wearing what I came to think of as "Dad" jeans and an ill-fitting plaid flannel shirt, I could tell he was lean and fairly muscular. And I discovered soon that I'd been mistaken about his eyes. They were a clear, true hazel, and very direct. My first impression of his smile had been dead on, though. It melted me every time it was aimed in my direction, making me grateful for the costume hiding my face and figure from his view!

Eventually, though, I emerged from my fuzzy camouflage to oversee an egg hunt in the food court on the afternoon of the day before Easter. Sure enough, just as things were getting started, Max and Ryan came into view. The boy raced off to join the throng of children.

I welcomed everyone, explained the rules of the hunt, and blew a whistle to signal the start. Much scampering and laughter followed as the kids began seeking the hundreds of eggs Janice and I had spent hours hiding that morning, before the mall opened. I stood back to watch with a sigh of relief, glad that the week was finally almost over.

"I almost didn't recognize you without your cute, fluffy tail," Ryan said, materializing out of nowhere beside me.

"My own mother wouldn't have known me in that suit!" I gaped at him, and then started to laugh. "How on earth did you know?"

"Your voice. It's unmistakable."

I blinked. "Really?"

"Umm hmm. So, the men around here are foolish as well as unfriendly?"

That made me laugh again. "I thought it was just me," I admitted.

Ryan shook his head. "No, sugar, it isn't you. These northerners have no idea how to treat a lady, that's all."

"Good to know." I lifted a brow at him. "Are you flirting with me?"

"If you need to ask, apparently I'm not very good at it."

I smiled. "Oh, you're good at it, all right."

"Does that mean you'll consider having a drink with me next Friday night?"

"Sorry. I don't date married men."

"Now, would I be asking if I were still married?" Ryan retorted, a wicked twinkle in his eyes.

"You aren't?"

"I think this conversation should wait until Friday, don't you? If you're saying yes, I mean."

I waited until I blew the whistle again to end the festivities to answer. "I definitely am," I said quietly.

We exchanged business cards, and then Ryan was off to collect Max. I watched him go, a little dazed by what had just happened.

It had been a long time since I'd had a date. Almost two years. And now I was having drinks with the most attractive man I'd met in all of that time in only a few days.

I had nothing to wear!

Of course, the fact that I had no idea where Ryan intended to take me didn't stop me from remedying that—and in a hurry. I bought three new dressy-casual outfits, had my hair trimmed, and gave myself a French manicure.

I was grateful for that when Ryan called on Wednesday night to confirm that we were still on for Friday.

"I thought we'd go to Kensington Manor, if that's agreeable to you," he said.

"Perfect." Nice, but laid-back enough that we'd be comfortable. Also, a short cab ride home, if things didn't go well. "Should I meet you there?"

"I'll pick you up at eight-thirty. Max is always asleep by eight, which will give me plenty of time."

"Fine. So, I'll see you then."

"G'bye, sugar."

I hung up and fanned myself. Sugar. Amazing what just one little word, uttered in a deep, silky voice, could do to a reasonably self-possessed woman like myself. Being so out of practice was probably partly to blame, but there was something about Ryan Dobson that had kept me off-balance from the start.

I hoped I wasn't playing with fire, but something told me I was.

The first ten minutes of my date with Ryan proved it.

When he knocked on my door, looking good enough to eat, I knew I was a goner.

No more "Dad" jeans for our date. Ryan was wearing well-cut charcoal gray slacks and a thin cotton sweater a couple of shades darker. Both emphasized the truth of what I'd been imagining about his body. He wasn't a bodybuilder, but he had lots of muscles— probably the result of honest work, rather than a gym membership.

"You look beautiful," Ryan said.

"Thank you." I made haste to put on my coat to hide the blush his words elicited and tucked my purse under my arm. "You clean up fairly well yourself."

He grinned. "Nice of you to notice."

"I may not get out much, but I do recognize an attractive man when I see one."

"Why is that?" Ryan asked, once he had me settled in his car.

"Sorry?"

"That you don't go out a lot?"

"Work keeps me busy. I have a lot of friends and family in the area."

"You're also not comfortable with receiving compliments."

"I don't get many." I looked out the window.

"Hard to believe, Paulette. A woman who looks like you…"

Something in Ryan's voice made me turn back toward him. "I'm nothing special."

"You are so wrong about that. You have no idea how lovely you are, do you? Or how amazed I am that you agreed to come out with me tonight?"

"Ryan. . . ."

"I couldn't believe it when you said yes. Seriously."

"You don't have to sweet-talk me."

Ryan smiled one of those incredible, breath-stealing smiles that I'd only previously witnessed close up while hidden inside the bunny suit.

"Yes, I do. You'll take some spoiling, sugar. And if you think that was sweet-talk, you haven't heard anything yet."

Kensington Manor is an old, classy hotel close to the airport. Couples of all ages filled the dimly lit room almost to capacity, their conversation rendered nearly inaudible by the soft music in the background.

Once we were seated at a cozy corner table, our drinks ordered, Ryan asked me if I'd had dinner. I confessed that I hadn't had time, so he asked the waiter if he'd bring us a menu.

While we waited, we chatted briefly about his job as a postal carrier—that explained the muscles, I figured—and then about Max, who'd apparently been excited to learn that Ryan's companion for the evening was "Miss Bunny."

"I don't get out much socially, either, but he was fine with it."

I took a sip of my mojito, digesting the information. "Surprising," I said finally.

"What makes you say that? My impressive conversational skills? Or maybe my smooth moves." Ryan pulled a face. "I haven't been on a date since Donna died, and I'll bet it shows."

Donna. Died.

I'd been expecting him to tell me he was divorced, maybe acrimoniously. The news that he was a widower hit me like a slap.

Impulsively, I touched his hand. "It doesn't," I said softly.

"You're a kind woman, Paulette." Ryan toyed with his beer, avoiding my eyes. "I'm sorry. I didn't mean to blurt it out like that."

"You have nothing to apologize for."

He smiled then . . . a sad smile. "You are a special woman, did you know that?"

"Someone whose opinion I'm starting to trust recently informed me of the fact." I took another swallow of mojito for courage. "How?"

"Complications from lupus. Eighteen months ago."

I had no idea what to say next. "I'm sorry" seemed ridiculous, since I didn't know Donna. Instead, I squeezed his hand and said, "Tell me about her."

"She was the strong one in our marriage. No matter what happened, how bad it got, she never let it stop her from living her life. Until the end." Ryan cleared his throat, and glanced at me. His eyes were very bright. "She was left-handed, she loved animals, and crazy action movies. Max was her miracle. Our miracle. Donna wasn't supposed to be able to have a baby, and yet there he was. Strong and healthy and perfect."

Tears stung my eyes. "He looks like her."

"Just like her. Right down to the shape of his fingernails and a birthmark on his back. He's left-handed, too. It's painful sometimes, but mostly it's a comfort." Ryan sighed. "Oh, my. Paulette, I am sorry. This isn't exactly first date conversation, is it?"

"No. But a therapist would have a field day with you."

That made him laugh, and the moment passed. Our snacks arrived and removed the need for further discussion for a few minutes as we dug in. I didn't get a respite for long, though.

"So, what's your story?" Ryan asked at last, dabbing at his lips with a napkin. "What's an amazing woman like you doing running free?"

"You make me sound like a wild mustang," I said, a trifle acidly.

He chuckled. "I think you are, a little bit. In the sense that you like your own company. And you're pretty convinced you don't need anyone in your life."

"Yes, that's true," I allowed.

"You don't chatter. Silence doesn't make you nervous. Your independence is obvious." Ryan shrugged a shoulder. "It's not much of a leap."

"You see a lot," I said.

"I have time on my hands. I spend it people watching, sometimes. They're interesting to me."

"People in general?" I asked.

"Yes. But you especially. I find you interesting."

"I'm not."

"What fool told you that falsehood?"

I smiled. "No one."

"So, there's no great love in your past?"

"Afraid not."

"Nobody else you're pining for?" Ryan persisted.

"No."

"I'm glad," he said softly.

I looked him in the eye then. "Why? I think you'd be up to the job."

"Which job is that?"

"Making me forget almost anyone."

Ryan reached across the table and took my hand as the waiter removed our plates. "That's probably the nicest thing anyone's ever said to me, sugar," he said, when we were alone again.

I was grateful for the low lighting, because, suddenly, my cheeks were on fire. "It's true," I whispered.

"Good to know." Ryan slowly laced his fingers through mine, making the simple act seem as intimate as a kiss. "So, tell me a little more about yourself."

I did, struggling not to let on how flustered I was by the innocent contact. I talked my way through another mojito while he ordered coffee. All too soon, we rose to leave, and shortly afterward, Ryan left me at my front door with a gentlemanly kiss on the cheek.

"I'll call you," he said, lifting a hand as he walked away.

As I got ready for bed, I had to wonder if he would. Or will Ryan's feelings about his late wife rush to the fore, and stop our relationship before it can truly begin?

I didn't wait long to find out. In fact, I was discussing the matter with my best friend, Cindy, on the telephone the next day when I heard the signal for another call coming in.

"I'll bet that's him now," she said.

"You're an eternal optimist. I'll call you back." I depressed the flash button and said, "Hello?"

"Hello, sugar. How are you this morning?"

"Glad I only had two drinks." I laughed. "I had a lovely time, by the way."

"So did I. Listen, I know it's short notice, but are you busy this evening?"

"No, I'm not. What did you have in mind?"

"A DVD and some good wine?"

"Sounds wonderful. What time?"

"Let's say eight-thirty?"

"That works. Should I bring anything?"

"Unnecessary. Let me give you directions."

I scribbled them down on the back of my phone bill and then hung up. After I'd filled Cindy in, I went back to doing laundry. It didn't dawn on me until I was putting the last load in the dryer that I was humming.

Yes, I'm definitely a goner!

Ryan was the perfect host, providing all of the necessities for an evening in—wine, Cheetos, and a selection of DVDs to choose from, including my favorites.

It was unfortunate that it all went to waste.

We kept a decorous distance between us for all of ten minutes. Then Ryan shifted toward me and put his arm around my shoulders. All at once, we were kissing. Unhurriedly, but with plenty of heat. That went on for a very long time. Just kissing. Like we were in high school and getting to know each other, with someone's parents in the next room. It was so hot that I could barely stand it!

Apparently, Ryan shared my opinion. His breathing was a little erratic when he drew back long enough to say, "You're killing me."

"I can leave if you like."

"Don't even think about it," Ryan whispered, his mouth muffling my laughter.

"This is crazy," I said, my lips pressed to his warm throat. The scent of his skin was driving me wild.

"This is amazing," Ryan contradicted.

"That, too."

We spent the following Saturday afternoon skating with Max, and I had a family dinner scheduled for Sunday. All Ryan and I really had time for was a few stolen kisses. The next few weeks flew by; soon we'd been dating for almost two months, and we still hadn't taken our physical relationship to the next level.

That was fine with me. Although I'd spoken the truth about lacking a forever kind of love in my past, I had made the mistake of jumping into things too quickly with men on several occasions. I didn't mind waiting to see if Ryan and I were compatible before we ended up in bed.

Not that I didn't want him. I did. And it was definitely mutual. But our timing always seemed to be off. When Max wasn't with us, other things intervened. I felt very close to Ryan emotionally, and he opened up to me, too, but we just couldn't seem to take the final step and become lovers.

The truth of the situation became obvious to me on the warm late spring day when we took Max to the zoo. It was meant to be an early sixth birthday gift for him; a party was planned for the day itself, which was two weeks later. The three of us had a wonderful day together, and then I went back to the apartment with them. Ryan and I cooked a meal, and then I read Max a bedtime story, as I'd recently begun to do when I'd spent time with him during the day. When I was done, I stood and leaned over to kiss his forehead, smoothing his hair before I got up.

"Are you going to be my mommy now?" he asked sleepily.

I froze, and glanced at Ryan.

"We'll talk about that in the morning. Go to sleep, buddy," he said, taking my hand and leading me out of the room.

Ryan and I cleaned up the kitchen in silence. I couldn't think of a single thing that made sense to say, so when we were through, I murmured, "I should go."

"Maybe that's best. I'll call you," he said, in a voice that I'd never heard before.

But he didn't call. Not the next day, and not in the week following.

"He didn't break up with you," Cindy insisted.

"Sure feels like it to me," I said. "You didn't see his face. He was horrified by it. Horrified by the idea that Max might be thinking of me as his mother."

"I'm sure you're overreacting." She pitched a pillow at my head. "You're a terrific woman, and you'd be a great mother. Ryan knows that."

I managed to duck out of the way, and snatched another brownie out of the pan on the coffee table. Chewing thoughtfully on a delicious bite of it, I said, "I'm not even positive I want kids."

"Did you tell Ryan that?"

"In the interests of full disclosure, I believe it did come up," I admitted.

"So, maybe he was afraid you would be upset."

I reached for my milk. "He was right," I said. "But not because of what Max said. Ryan's not over Donna. That much I know for sure."

"He wants to move on, but he can't."

"Making me Transition Girl yet again."

"It's your sweet nature and nurturing manner," she teased. "Seriously, do you want this guy? I mean, do you really want him?"

"Not if he's still living in the past, with his dead wife." I shook my head vigorously. "It's all or nothing."

"So, tell him. Call him, go and see him. Whatever it takes. Lay it on the line."

"I'm not sure I can."

"Then forget it. Go back to being a . . . what was it? Wild mustang?" Cindy asked.

I threw the pillow back at her, and had the satisfaction of seeing it hit her squarely in the middle of her chest.

"Shut up," I ordered, but she didn't hear me. She was too busy laughing at me, with the comforting callousness of an old and dear friend.

Max's birthday celebration was being held in the party room in Ryan's apartment building, and, judging by the noise traveling down the hall from the open door, there was quite a crowd inside. Maybe I'd have the chance to leave the gift I'd brought, wish the sweet little guy a happy birthday, and escape before Ryan even knew I'd been there.

I was banking on it, but like most things in my life the scheme didn't work out as I'd planned.

I found Max without difficulty—he was wearing a silver foil cowboy hat and a bright red T-shirt with Birthday Cowboy emblazoned on the front of it. He squealed with delight when he saw me, ran over, and gave me a big hug.

"I told Daddy you'd come, 'cause you promised!" he announced. "Grandma Beatrice! Grandma Beatrice! C'mere!"

I opened my mouth to say that I couldn't stay when an attractive, silver-haired lady answered his summons. She had to be Donna's mother.

"Beatrice Connolly," she said, offering me her hand. Her brilliant blue eyes were filled with good humor and curiosity.

"Paulette Snow," I replied, taking it.

"You're a friend of Ryan's?" Beatrice asked.

"This is Miss Bunny," Max said helpfully.

Beatrice's silver eyebrows lifted. "Definitely a friend of Ryan's," she said firmly. "He's just stepped out to get some more ice. You'll wait?"

"I can't. I just wanted to wish Max a happy birthday." I smiled at her. "It was nice meeting you, Mrs. Connolly."

"Are you sure you can't stay?"

I nodded, hugged Max again, and kissed his rosy cheek. "Love you, bud," I said. "See you soon."

I turned away and started toward the door just as Ryan walked in, hauling two big bags of ice. I watched as my presence registered on his face. I made a break for it when he headed for the table where the refreshments were arranged.

I made it as far as the parking lot before Ryan caught up to me.

"Paulette, wait. Please."

"There's nothing to say now, Ryan."

"It means a lot to me that you came today. You really are special."

"So you've said. Maybe your next girlfriend can help you figure out how you really feel about me." I shook my head. "We could've had something great, Ryan. We really could've. But I wasn't enough for you, was I?"

"Is that what you think?"

"I think you're still in love with Donna."

Ryan flinched. "I am. I guess always will be. She was my first love, the mother of my son. But she's gone. And you're here."

"I am. Standing right in front of you, saying I want to try to work things out, but only if you're not going to hold back any more. So, what are you going to do about it? Let me walk away?"

"No." Ryan took a step toward me. "I hurt you, Paulette. I'm sorry for that. Max caught me off-guard that night. Let me try to make it up to you."

"I'm not sure you can."

Ryan pulled me into his arms. His lips were cool at first, but warmed as he kissed me again and again.

"Come back inside," he said softly, after a long moment of charged silence.

"I can't. It's family time, and I'd be intruding."

"Tonight, then?"

It was a question, but it was also a promise.

Ryan and I finally became lovers on that balmy, spring night. I'd never experienced passion like his before. In a way, I was glad we'd waited, because being apart from him after knowing how it could be with us would have been miserable.

Despite our closeness, we continued to take some aspects of our relationship one day at a time. I knew I could never replace Donna, and I was at peace with that. I was also aware that Ryan was still grieving his loss and afraid of making a deeper commitment because of it. But he was doing his best to overcome both grief and fear, and that was all I really hoped for.

I also came to love Max like he was my own son. Safe in my love for Ryan, encouraged by the strength of my bond with Max, I decided that more children, some day, might be a wonderful idea.

When Ryan did ask me to marry him almost two years later, I said yes before he finished his sentence. I put my arms around him and cried. Because by then, there was no way even I could fail to see that he'd taken my "all or nothing" condition to heart. Ryan, Max, and I were finally a family. And we always will be, no matter what else our future together held.

THE END

www.ingramcontent.com/pod-product-compliance
Lightning Source LLC
Chambersburg PA
CBHW071412170626
46811CB00003B/1361